The Second Best Pony

BOOK 2

The Second Best Pony

By Helen Haraldsen

The Second Best Pony

Copyright © 2019 to Helen Haraldsen

www.helenharaldsen.co.uk

This book is a work of fiction based on the author's life. Any resemblance to any other persons, living or dead, is purely coincidental.

Cover Design, editing, and formatting by Let's Get Booked: www.letsgetbooked.com

Print ISBN: 978-1-9160112-5-0

eBook ISBN: 978-1-9160112-6-7

Second edition with minor changes

Contents

This book is dedicated to the Fell pony; a beautiful, tough and versatile breed who was the first to introduce me to the world of ponies and horses. From their beginnings as pit ponies and packhorses, they can now be found showing, jumping, carriage driving, pleasure, and endurance riding.

As best friends go, there can be no better friend than a Fell pony.

- One -

Starting Again

Amber Anderson's stomach clenched like an angry fist. She wasn't sure whether it was nerves or excitement that was pummelling her insides as she rode her black Fell pony, Pearl, around the perimeter of the Pony Club field, waiting for the first rally of the new season to begin.

Amber had joined Blakefield Pony Club the previous year, but she'd had a disastrous time; being humiliated at her first rally; and getting eliminated from her debut round of show jumping. And of course, there was the fun ride which had ended in disaster after a terrible accident.

A sudden blast of chill April breeze sent an icy tingle down Amber's spine as she remembered that awful time.

Amber felt alone without her friend Joanne beside her. Joanne and her pony, Flash, were both still recovering from the injuries they sustained in the accident the previous summer and would probably miss the whole season. Amber yearned for a friend to ride around with as there was someone she dreaded seeing. However, glancing around the car park, she was relieved to see that Elisha Templeton's imposing blue and yellow horsebox was also missing. The problem with Elisha was that she was cruel, spoilt and nasty and was partly responsible for Joanne's accident. Last year, she had also said some very unkind things about Pearl, making Amber apprehensive about seeing her again.

She scanned the field and noticed a long-legged girl mounting a flea-bitten grey pony of about 14.2hh. The girl gathered up her reins and urged her pony into a reluctant walk. Deciding she'd had enough of being on her own, Amber took a deep breath and rode over to introduce herself.

The grey pony flicked her ears back and raised a hind leg threateningly as Pearl drew up alongside her. Fearing the pony might lash out, Amber hurriedly steered Pearl out of kicking range.

"Oh, I'm *so* sorry," gasped the girl, seeing Amber's startled reaction. "She's so unfriendly. I'm really sorry she tried to kick you," she apologised sincerely.

Amber had been about to tell her that ponies prone to kicking should wear a red ribbon in their tails to warn other riders to give them a wide berth, but seeing the girl was genuinely sorry and upset, she changed her mind.

"It's okay, don't worry. I just came over to say hello. Are you a new member?"

"Yeah, I've just joined. I'm really nervous." She smiled shyly, her round brown eyes giving her face a startled expression. "I've only been riding for a year and just got Sable at Christmas. Everyone looks so good." She looked towards the older riders who were working their horses in controlled circles of collected canter. "I've never jumped before. I'm bound to be a total disaster and fall off in front of everyone."

Amber laughed. "That's just how I felt at my first rally, but they put you in groups, so you'll be riding with people at a similar level to yourself. I'm Amber, by the way," she added, realising she hadn't introduced herself.

"I'm Natalie," she replied.

"Oh, look, they're ready to start," said Amber, catching sight of Mrs Best, the Pony Club DC waving at them. "Let's go and see which group we're in."

- Two -

Trouble Already

Amber patted Pearl's damp, curly neck and slid gratefully from the saddle at the end of the rally. She hadn't worked so hard since her lessons last year. She had been in Geraldine's group – the young, exuberant instructor she'd had for her one and only rally last year. There were four groups; the first for very young or inexperienced riders, with the following three groups comprising of progressively older and more experienced riders. Amber remembered with a cringe how she had ridden into the third group at her first rally, assuming she would be with riders of eleven to thirteen years of age as she was eleven herself then. But because of her lack of experience and Pearl not matching up to the other ponies' abilities, she had been moved into the second group of eight to ten-year-olds, and Elisha had laughed at her.

After a lot of lessons and hard work with Pearl since last year, Amber was delighted to find that she had been promoted to the third group. As she proudly trotted towards the group, she was surprised, and a little annoyed, to see that Natalie was following her. She'd assumed the new girl would be in one of the lower groups due to her lack of experience, just as *she* had been last year.

They joined a girl called Kate on a young bay horse, and another girl with dark curly hair called Emily who rode Fudge, a chunky chestnut gelding. She looked familiar. Amber thought she recognised her from school, but she wasn't in her year group.

They had started with some flatwork that really got their muscles aching, and then Geraldine had shown them how to give the correct aids for a turn on the forehand. Amber, Emily and Kate had managed quite good turns, with Pearl being particularly co-operative for a change. Poor Natalie, on the other hand, had a terrible time. She listened carefully to Geraldine's instructions and gave the aids clearly, but Sable seemed to be willfully disobedient. Instead of simply moving her hindquarters around her front feet in a half turn as was being asked, she laid her ears back, shook her head in annoyance, backed up and finally did a mini rear which resulted in Natalie tuning ghostly white and looking close to tears.

"Right, I think we've all had enough of that now!" Geraldine exclaimed, seeing that Natalie was shaken. "Let's have a change."

As Geraldine dragged some poles out to lie on the ground as trotting poles, Amber looked forward to showing off Pearl's improved jumping skills. Last year Pearl had been very reluctant to jump and would either just stop in front of the fence or dodge around it, rather than go over it. Mrs Anderson had endured a particularly painful experience while jumping in the field at Shaw Farm, where the ponies were kept.

Amber had been trying to get Pearl to jump some blue barrels pushed together to make a wall, but Pearl had other ideas and just kept refusing at the last minute. An exasperated Mrs Anderson had decided to take over and she mounted Pearl to 'teach her a lesson.' Feeling the increased strength and confidence of her new rider, Pearl realised she needed to employ new tactics to continue getting her own way. Mrs Anderson rode smartly around the small paddock, giving Pearl very definite aids to show her that she meant business. Sure that Pearl had got the message, Mrs Anderson turned her towards the blue barrels and coaxed her into a canter. "Come on Pearlipops," she urged the pony. Pearl cantered gaily towards the jump, ears pricked, looking for all the world like she was going to follow through, when at the very last second she simultaneously shoved her head down between her knees, dropped her left shoulder, twisted to the right and gave a little buck. Sitting on the fence, watching, Amber's hands flew to her face and she pressed them against her cheeks, almost covering her eyes as she realised, almost in slow-motion, the inevitable landing place of her mother.

Pearl careered away, and Mrs Anderson, all balance lost, flew head-first into a large patch of stinging nettles. Pearl stopped, snatched a mouthful of grass to munch, then looked up, ears pricked quizzically to admire her handiwork.

The naughty pony could not be smug about her antics for long, however, as Mrs Anderson emerged from the nettle patch like the Incredible Hulk. She hadn't turned green (apart from the fronds of nettle hanging from her hat); she was red-faced, her arms and hands covered in hot stinging pimples, her fists balled at her sides. Catching Pearl up, she remounted and booted her back towards the barrel jump. This time, the pony didn't dare resist her rider as she felt the suppressed rage travelling down the reins. So, with grass still sticking out of her mouth and her eyes wide with surprise at losing the battle, Pearl had jumped the barrels three times before Mrs Anderson flung herself out of the saddle, chucked the reins at Amber and strode away, head held high.

Then there was Amber's first show last year where she had been eliminated at the fourth fence in her first round of show jumping. After that, her parents decided she wouldn't do any more competing until she'd had some lessons.

Now, with months of lessons behind her, Amber felt much happier about jumping. Pearl had eventually realised it was easier to jump on the first attempt, as if she refused, she would only be made to keep going. So, always wanting an easy life, Pearl had become a reliable, albeit slow jumper, as long as the poles didn't get too high. Amber couldn't wait to see if Pearl would still be as good since her winter break from lessons.

"Right everyone," called Geraldine, wiping the mud off her hands, "shorten your stirrups and trot steadily down through the poles. Concentrate on keeping a steady rhythm and an even tempo. And don't look down," she added with a chuckle.

All three ponies and Kate's young horse managed the poles well, with Natalie going last so that Sable could follow the others.

Natalie's ashen face returned to its normal colour, and she smiled happily as Sable plonked over the poles.

Geraldine then raised the last pole to make a low jump and asked the riders to continue trotting down but be prepared for the fence at the end, remembering to go into jumping position over it. This task suited Pearl perfectly as she preferred to jump from trot.

"Well done Amber," nodded Geraldine as she went first down the line and over the jump perfectly. "You go next, Emily."

Emily brought Fudge round and did a good job of steadying him. As there was now a jump at the end, he tried to canter and got rather unbalanced as Emily brought him back to a trot. By the time he got to the fence, Emily had steadied him well and he produced a very neat jump.

"Well ridden, Emily," Geraldine praised, clapping her hands. "You can do it again in a minute, just to make sure he doesn't try to rush. Okay, Natalie." She signalled to the girl to come and take her turn.

Sable headed up the poles in a rather sluggish trot, but as soon as she saw the jump she quickly spun away, just like Pearl had done with Mrs Anderson, flinging Natalie up out of the saddle and on to her neck. Natalie clutched at the pony's mane tightly as she wriggled and pushed herself back into the saddle before desperately trying to recover her stirrups. Fortunately, Geraldine had sprung forward and caught Sable by the bridle to stop her from charging away. But for the instructor's quick actions, Natalie would surely have come off.

"Whoops! Nearly!" exclaimed Geraldine lightly. "I think we'll let you follow someone this time."

"Er... right," muttered Natalie, looking rather flustered.

Amber knew she was probably feeling frightened and embarrassed. After all, she'd had the same trouble with Pearl last year.

Kate had a quick turn with no trouble, then Geraldine summoned Emily to go over the poles again ahead of Natalie, to give her a lead.

"Put your leg on and really ride her forward more this time," Geraldine instructed. "Use your legs and reins to keep her straight. Wake her up out of her daydream. Be positive," she commanded encouragingly.

This time, Natalie followed closely behind Emily. Fudge, now knowing he had to trot through the poles, went perfectly. Sable followed him quite eagerly, and as she neared the jump, Natalie steeled herself and squeezed with her legs. This time, however, Sable wasn't taken by surprise and knew exactly what to expect. Just as Natalie was beginning to lean forward to adopt the jumping position, Sable put her head right down and stopped dead in her tracks. Natalie was catapulted out of the saddle, slid over Sable's withers, and crashed head-first into the jump. Finding herself free at last, the grey pony hurtled across the field, bucking madly with stirrups, reins, and clods of earth flying.

That was where the rally ended. Natalie had banged her head and hurt her neck. Her dad had left her sitting on the ramp of their trailer, wrapped in a warm horse blanket, while he and Geraldine went to try and catch Sable. This proved an impossible task, as she had no intention of going home, and trotted away as soon as they got close to her. Eventually, after causing so much chaos and disturbing the other groups so much that everyone had to give up, a whole troop of adults encircled and caught the pony.

Red-faced with embarrassment, Natalie's dad flopped wearily onto the ramp beside his daughter. Amber and Mr Anderson finished brushing Pearl, hung up her haynet, and went over to see if Natalie was okay.

Geraldine was there untacking the ungrateful pony, whose ears were flat back, her eyes rolling as she tried to fight against her short rope to bite Geraldine as she loosened the girth. Unperturbed, Geraldine ignored her and carried on, flashing Amber a smile as she walked past.

Natalie had removed her hat. Her short blonde hair was damp and tousled, plastered to her pale, clammy face.

"Uuuurgh," she groaned, rubbing the back of her neck, her eyes half-closed as she slumped against her dad on the ramp.

"Hi, Andrew Anderson," said Amber's dad, holding out his hand to the man on the ramp, "is there anything we can do to help? Could we take your pony and drop her off for you?" he offered, thinking Natalie would need a trip to the hospital to get checked out.

Natalie's dad looked up with pale blue eyes and shook his head. "Thanks for the offer," he said, standing and shaking Mr Anderson's hand, "but that devil won't travel with another pony. I think one accident is enough for today." He sighed and looked drained. "My wife is coming to take Natalie to the doctor, and I'll get that thing home." He nodded towards Sable, now booted and bandaged, ready to go, but looking as grumpy as ever. "Thanks again."

As Amber sat in the car while they drove back to the farm, she couldn't help wondering what the year would bring. Last year had ended in disaster and this year had begun with one. *Surely things will start getting better,* she hoped.

– Three –

A New Friend

It was two weeks before Amber saw Emily and Natalie again at the Easter Monday gymkhana. Blakefield Pony Club had long held the tradition of hosting the first local outdoor show of the year, and it was always well attended despite the fact that it was often plagued with April showers and cold winds – the field being situated close to the coast made it rather exposed to the weather.

The location did have its advantages to compensate; the field was large and flat with good drainage, so the going was always good and there was a magnificent view of the surrounding countryside. The field was sandwiched between the distant mountains of the Lake District, undulating valleys flecked with the purple and gold of heather and gorse, a patchwork of farmland, and the nearby coast of St

Bees. It was a truly spectacular setting. But as spring was only creeping cautiously into the land with its painted fingers dabbing colour everywhere, the greys and browns of winter were not yet forgotten.

It was an unusually warm, pleasant day. Earthy smells of dewy grass, soft mud and hay were occasionally pierced by the sharper scents of hoof oil, coat gloss and boot polish as riders mounted their freshly bathed ponies for the equitation class.

Amber unloaded Pearl and was getting her ready - with some help from Mrs Anderson – for her own class of equitation, when a huge blue lorry with a striking yellow stripe like a lightning flash pulled on to the field. Amber could see Elisha Templeton's condescending face smirking down at her from the grand height of the cab as they drove by. Amber scowled and got back to brushing baby oil through Pearl's tail to make it shiny.

Although Elisha had momentarily admitted some remorse for last year's accident and had (or at least her parents had) sent a huge bouquet of flowers and expensive Belgian chocolates to Joanne, she had not phoned or visited once. And now, judging by the haughty smirk she had directed at Amber, she had no intention of reforming her character.

The reason for her smugness soon became evident as the ramp of their lorry was lowered and its passenger emerged. It was not a pony, but a small black horse of about 15.2hh. He was heavily rugged to protect his clipped body, but still, his quality could not be missed. Exquisitely formed, he stopped as his feet touched the grass and lifted his head up sharply to take in his new surroundings. His nostrils quivered as he snorted and shook his head, and the muscles of his beautiful dark face twitched uneasily as he inhaled the new smells of this unfamiliar environment.

Elisha looked delighted with herself as she saw heads turn and eyes lock on to the magnificent creature by her side. Determined to show off even more, she yanked the lead-rope sharply and walked forward. Still gazing around nervously, the horse was startled by Elisha's sudden, rough movement and skittered forward, bumping into her and nearly knocking her flat. Elisha staggered and righted herself quickly, smoothing her dark hair and glancing around furtively to see if anyone had noticed. Everyone looked away politely, pretending not to have seen, while

Amber giggled gleefully as she thought how Elisha had nearly swallowed and choked on her own conceited grin as the horse jolted her.

Do her good to be embarrassed for once, thought Amber.

The previous class was almost over, with the judge lining riders up to be presented with their rosettes, as Amber finished warming Pearl up. Other competitors for the class were congregating as the lap of honour cantered out of the equitation area amidst flapping rosette ribbons and beaming faces.

Amber could see other competitors riding towards her: Natalie on a neatly plaited Sable, who looked as ill-tempered as ever; a boy on a pretty dun pony; another, slightly plump boy on a piebald with blue eyes and a cute handlebar moustache; and Elisha. Amber looked around, noting Emily's absence. She'd heard her say she was coming at the rally.

The five riders followed each other around the marked area in a circle while they waited for the judge to return from collecting a score sheet and rosettes for their class.

Elisha rode her mount alongside Amber who had to look up to see the girl as she was so far above her.

"What do you think?" asked Elisha, looking down at Amber with raised eyebrows.

Amber knew she was talking about the horse, but she had a sudden urge to reply with tremendous wit and sarcasm, something like, "*I think about a lot of things Elisha, could you be more specific?*" but her courage failed her under the hard expectant weight of Elisha's eyes. Knowing exactly what she'd meant, Amber replied meekly. "He's really beautiful. What's he called?"

"Thunder Cat. He's fabulously well bred. His sire, Storm Cat is North America's top stallion. He's the sire of over fifty stakes winners worldwide and his stud fee is almost half a million dollars. His dam is a Grade A show-jumper. My dad found him through some of his contacts in the States and had him imported for me for Christmas. He was *so* expensive." Elisha's eyes glistened as she uttered the word 'expensive.' "We can't turn him out – he's stabled all the time unless he's led out in hand for some grass. We're going to be aiming him at top level eventing. We'll be training with the top people and I'm hoping to get him to the BE Under Eighteen Regional Team Championships in the summer."

"Oh right," said Amber, impressed both with the horse's credentials and Elisha's ability to remember and recite it like a well-practised script. At the same time, she wondered why such a grand horse aimed at the prestigious heights of three-day eventing was entered in an insignificant equitation class at a local Pony Club gymkhana. Something of her thoughts must have shown on her face as Elisha hurriedly went on to explain her reasons for being there.

"Of course, he's *way* above these poxy little Pony Club affairs, but we thought we'd let him see things locally before he goes anywhere important. He's only five, and we wouldn't want him to show us up. Besides, it'll do him good to have some wins under his belt when people ask what he's done."

Amber wasn't shocked by Elisha's confidence or at her disdain for small, local shows. *That's what comes from having the money to buy the best and the connections to get your own way*, she thought. Last year, Amber would have envied Elisha and her super-duper new winning machine, but she had since realised how lucky she was to have Pearl, with whom she shared a special bond. Even though she knew she would never win competitions with her, she still loved her, and that made her feel richer than Elisha, who saw her ponies only as a means to success rather than as friends.

She leant forward to stroke some stray strands of mane back into place as the judge returned and Elisha rode smoothly onto the track ahead of her.

***

After completing her own individual show and watching everyone else's, Amber's prediction as to the places was confirmed by the judge. Elisha was first on Thunder Cat, who, for a young horse, was already well-schooled and performed his show with grace, athleticism and control. The boy on the dun pony, who had also given a nice performance, was second. Amber was third, the boy on the moustached piebald was fourth – he had done quite well except that he'd cantered a full circle on the wrong leg without noticing – and Natalie was fifth as Sable had been totally uncooperative, slugged around like a plank of wood then refused point-blank to canter.

As the line of riders left the equitation area, preceded by Elisha, Amber noticed Emily was standing watching them. Instantly recognisable by her thick curly dark hair, she was wearing jeans and a white t-shirt emblazoned with a jubilant Mickey Mouse. She followed Amber back to the trailer and congratulated her on her third place. Her manner was so relaxed and easy, anyone would have thought they knew each other well, not that this was the first time they'd spoken to each other.

"Aren't you riding?" asked Amber, sitting down on the ramp and loosening her tie from its strangling hold on her neck.

"No. I just came to watch. Fudge came in from the field the other day with a really hot, swollen leg. I cold hosed it and bandaged an ice pack to it, but it didn't get any better, so we got the vet out. She reckons he's twisted it while running around in the field, so he has to have box rest for a few weeks. He's not enjoying it at all. He hates being kept in. I've hung some carrots up for him to play with, but he's not interested. Every time I go in the stable, he looks at me as if it's my fault. He makes me feel so guilty," Emily laughed, sitting down next to Amber. "So, no riding for me for the next few weeks." She finished, pulling a hay stalk out of her curls, suddenly looking glum.

Amber had an idea. "You could come and ride with me," she suggested, tentatively. We've got another Fell pony called Honey. You could come with us after school. You go to Wallam Academy like me, don't you? You're in Year Eight? I'll ask my dad if you want?"

"Yeah, thanks," Emily smiled, her hazel eyes twinkling, "that would be brill." Amber smiled back, pleased that Emily had agreed so enthusiastically.

The day stayed warm as the show progressed. Pearl went clear in her jumping round but then had two poles down in the jump-off when the fences were raised. She was doing so much better than last year, but she still lacked the energy and power to jump anything bigger than eighty centimetres; her absolute maximum.

She won the handy pony, which was becoming Pearl's forte as it required the pony to be steady and unfazed by the obstacles, and she had also tried games again, but Pearl totally lacked the competitive spirit required to race the other ponies, and firmly insisted on trotting all the way through the mug, flag, and ball and bucket races

Amber and Emily had watched dismally as Mr Riley led Sable away after she was eliminated at the first jump. The pony had refused to even enter the show jumping arena, and then, after being dragged in by Mr Riley, had reared one after another until Natalie was in floods of tears. She'd spent the rest of the time before they left sitting red-eyed in the car, refusing to come out even when Emily asked if she wanted to come and walk around with her.

Elisha had cleaned up as usual. As well as winning the equitation, she also won the ninety-centimetre and one metre pony show jumping classes on North Quest (who had stood so quietly in the lorry until it was his turn that Amber had not realised he was there). Then she won the ninety-centimetre horse class on Thunder Cat and came second in the metre class after a little mistake in the jump-off. Amber couldn't believe the young horse was jumping Opens already. But what he lacked in experience and training, he made up for through sheer ability. Even Amber, with her untrained eyes and non-existent knowledge of 'good breeding,' could see he was a quality horse. He had it all: amazing presence, a huge bold jump and an impeccable temperament. Despite the racing blood coursing through his veins and his youthful energy and exuberance, he was a perfect gentleman for his slight thirteen-year-old rider.

The horse classes finished and the members who had stayed until the end helped to take the jumps down and store them away in the container.

"Do you need a lift home?" Mr Anderson asked Emily, seeing that she was alone, and everyone was leaving the field.

"Oh thanks, but my mum will be on her way now. I phoned her ten minutes ago."

"Dad," asked Amber, suddenly remembering her earlier conversation with Emily, "Emily's pony is lame at the moment, so she can't ride. Could she come to the farm with us one day after school and ride Honey out with me?"

Mr Anderson immediately agreed, and it was decided that if it was okay with Emily's parents, she would go with them to Shaw Farm on Wednesday after school.

"See you on Wednesday then," said Amber happily.

"I'll see you at school tomorrow and let you know if it's okay," Emily replied, just as a small blue car pulled into the field, driven by a smiling woman wearing a headscarf with paint all over her nose and forehead. Emily waved as she ran towards the car. "Looks like Mum's been decorating," she called. "See you tomorrow!"

"Bye!" cried Amber, waving madly, pleased to have made a new friend.

– Four –

Honey's Surprise

At quarter past three on Wednesday, Amber went to the music block to meet Emily after her last lesson. She waited a few minutes until the increasing volume of chatter indicated that the Year Eights were on their way out. Emily emerged, talking and laughing with her friends and didn't even see Amber waiting beside the door. She stopped a little way off and continued talking animatedly, her curls bouncing as she threw back her head to laugh at something a tall blond boy had said. He grinned as Emily wiped the tears of laughter away and pushed him jokingly with one hand.

Amber wondered if she'd forgotten about riding and felt nervous about approaching the older group. She sidled over, trying not to look conspicuous, hoping to catch Emily's eye without the others noticing her.

"Amber! Hey!" The plan worked. Emily spotted her, but then waved her over. Everyone turned to look as Amber reluctantly joined them.

"Is this your little pony friend then?" The blond boy asked. Everyone laughed. Amber blushed and looked down uncomfortably.

"Shut up, Paul," Emily chuckled. "Just ignore him." She put her arm around Amber and steered her away, calling back over her shoulder. "He so fancies himself!"

"Not as much as you fancy me," he retorted, blowing a kiss to Emily, who snorted and shook her head.

"Sorry about that," Emily fell into step next to Amber as they walked to the car, "he's okay but sometimes he can be a pain."

"Is he your boyfriend?" Amber asked shyly.

"God *no*," Emily exclaimed, "The only man in my life is my little Fudgey. How could I love anyone else?"

Both girls arrived at the car in fits of giggles and were still spluttering as they fastened their seatbelts. Mrs

Anderson raised an eyebrow but decided not to ask as she pulled out of school to head for the farm.

***

"She's lovely," Emily said softly as she ran her fingers through Honey's copper streaked black mane. "So gentle."

Honey was indeed a gentle pony. Where cheeky Pearl would sometimes give Amber a shove with her head or use her to scratch on when she was itchy, or 'accidentally' stand on Amber's toes when she wasn't looking, Honey was a complete angel. She would lower her head to be bridled, pick up her own feet to be cleaned out and never shoved, pushed or stood on anybody. Her only fault was that she sometimes wouldn't let Mr Anderson catch her, although Amber and her mum never had any trouble.

"Are you sure you don't mind me riding her, Mrs Anderson?" Emily asked politely. "I feel bad that you're going to be sitting around here while I'm riding your pony."

"Oh, don't worry pet. I've brought my book. I'll be quite happy," replied Mrs Anderson, "and I can give Kasper a little walk."

"Ohhhhh," Amber groaned, "I'm surprised she even remembered to come and pick us up if she's reading a book."

Emily's eyebrows rose questioningly. Amber laughed, "The world stops when Mum's reading a book – she doesn't move, she doesn't make tea, she doesn't even go to the loo - she just sits there till she's read it from start to finish. I hope you don't mind sleeping in the stable tonight, as we'll never be able to move her once she's got going. She'll forget we're even here." Amber gave her mother a playful elbow.

Mrs Anderson narrowed her eyes and pursed her lips, though Amber knew she was suppressing a smile. "I'm not *that* bad. I'll definitely get you home…sometime before midnight," she added playfully. They all laughed.

The afternoon was chilly as the girls rode through the silent forestry, the great ominous looking trees sheltering them from the icy gusts of wind that blew through the valley. Amber enjoyed the ride as she and Emily chatted easily about ponies, homework, teachers, music and everything under the sun, until the conversation turned to the show on Monday.

"Natalie's pony seems a bit of a horror, doesn't she?" commented Emily, "I mean, she doesn't want to do anything except argue and fight. I wonder if there's something wrong with Sable or if she really is just bad-tempered and nasty."

"I don't know," Amber replied, picturing Sable's face with ears laid back and teeth bared. "I read somewhere that there are no bad horses, just bad people who ruin them, but Natalie and her dad seem like nice, kind people to me."

"Yeah. Maybe Sable's had a bad experience in the past and it's ruined her, but you'd think Natalie'd have seen her bad temper when they tried her. I don't know why anyone would buy a pony like that, especially when she's so unsuitable for Natalie – 'cause she's inexperienced and a bit nervous. That pony will ruin her confidence and she'll give up before the end of the year I think, if they don't sell it and get her something else."

"You can't just sell a pony and get a new one though!" protested Amber, still shocked at people's ability to regard a pony as just a belonging like an old toy that can be passed on and replaced with a better one without a thought.

"Sometimes it's the best thing to do," Emily replied, looking serious. "If a horse and rider aren't right for each other, they just make each other unhappy, and that's no good for either of them. For the person, keeping a horse you don't like is an expensive way of making yourself miserable, and you could also get hurt." Amber thought back to when she had considered that Pearl was not the pony for her. Emily continued. "Also, it must be stressful for the horse when their owner doesn't understand them – after all, they can't tell us what they want from us to make them happy – their ideas might be different from ours. Sometimes a combination is better off being separated and both find they are much happier with someone else. Natalie would be much happier with another pony, and you never know, Sable might be better tempered with someone else."

"I've never thought of it like that before," said Amber, thinking how sensible Emily's words were. "I suppose it's like people – some you love, some you like, some you can tolerate but there's some you just can't help disliking -

sometimes you don't even know why you don't like them. It's weird."

Emily nodded. "That's right, those people who you don't like but don't know why – they haven't done or said anything nasty to you, but still you can't get on – can be because you are just too different. You have different personalities and characters that just don't match. And that can happen with people and horses too. Natalie and Sable obviously can't click together, so why struggle on? I mean, if you started going out with a lad and found you didn't like him, would you carry on or would you find someone you liked who made you happy?"

"Yeah, good point." Amber laughed at Emily's rather grown-up comparison, and thought how she would hate it if she had to go out with someone like Robert from her form group. He picked his nose when he thought no-one was looking, talked with his mouth full, and stared at people in a very unsettling manner. She could understand how she would be very bad-tempered and unhappy if she spent much time in his company.

"Whereas, what would you *give* to have Elisha's new horse? Pfwoar!" Emily said, changing the subject.

"I know what you mean. Her parents must be seriously loaded. She told me his sire's stud fee was nearly half a million dollars!"

"That's unbelievable," Emily scoffed, "I think she's exaggerating there."

"No. I looked him up on the internet – it's true."

"Wow," breathed Emily, awestruck. "Now, I totally adore my Freaky Treacle but what I wouldn't give to have a horse like Thunder Cat. Elisha is *so* lucky."

"*Freaky Treacle?* What's that?" Asked Amber incredulously.

"Oh, that's Fudge's show name," Emily explained, grinning mischievously.

"That's such a cool name!" Amber managed to get out before she exploded with giggles.

The rest of the ride was punctuated with frequent outbursts of laughter, and by the time they got back to the farm track, their sides and faces were aching from laughing so much.

As they rode past Joanne's house, Amber habitually looked over the gate as she rode by and was surprised but pleased to see Joanne coming down the path from the field, leading a pale palomino pony beside her.

"Jo," she called, standing up in her stirrups and waving so she could be seen now that they had ridden alongside the tall hedge that bordered Joanne's house.

Joanne looked up and waved back. "Come in," she called.

Amber hopped off Pearl and opened the gate for Emily and herself to enter the yard. Turning around, she saw that Joanne had tied the pony up and was waiting for them. Amber led Pearl towards the stables and smiled warmly at Joanne, noticing that her blonde bob had grown out to shoulder length. "I'm pleased to see you're out and about again," she said sincerely, "and is this your new pony?"

"Yeah, this is Merry." Joanne stroked the milky coat as she introduced the pony. "She's a Welsh Arab cross, 14.2hh and eight years old, but she hasn't done much except breed a foal. Mum got her quite cheap at an auction – she knew the seller – they told her Merry was really nice, just inexperienced. They were happy to sell her to Mum because they knew her, without Merry even going

35

in the ring. Mum thought she'd make a nice project for me this summer to just bring on and maybe take to a couple of competitions towards the end of the year. She's sweet, isn't she?"

The mare was indeed very pretty. She had the definite Arab dished face with a broad forehead tapering into a small, delicate muzzle. Her coat was a smooth, creamy colour like vanilla ice-cream, lightened further by a long white flowing mane and tail, four white socks and a blaze on her face.

"I was just going to take her in the field and do some little jumps. You two are welcome to come in and jump too if you like."

Amber checked her watch, concerned that her mum would want to get home. Then she remembered she was reading her book and stopped worrying about the time.

"Do you want to do some jumping?" she asked Emily.

"Yeah, great," came the enthusiastic reply.

"Okay, but Honey hasn't done any jumping and she can be a bit of a wimp."

"That's fine, we'll just play."

"Oh, do you two know each other?" gasped Amber, realising that she hadn't introduced Emily and Joanne and the latter was probably wondering who the stranger was.

"Yes, we know each other through the club. We've competed against each other a few times, although Fudge has never managed to beat Flash, obviously," Emily said, turning to face Joanne. "I was sorry to hear about your accident. How is Flash?"

"Well, he doesn't look too bad – he healed up okay, but he still isn't totally sound. I think he's just putting it on so he can carry on enjoying an easy life."

Soon the girls were in the small paddock warming up over trotting poles and small cross poles. Joanne's mum came out to help and watched her daughter anxiously as she popped Merry over the small jumps.

"Okay love?" she asked. Her tone was light, but her furrowed brow betrayed her concern.

"Yes, Mum, stop worrying, I'm fine. She doesn't pull at all and she's enjoying herself," Joanne said, giving her pony a pat on the neck.

Sensing that her daughter didn't want her fussing about her, Mrs Jones turned her attention to Amber and Emily.

"It's nice to see you girls. Jo's only doing little jumps with Merry as she's so green, but we've got some new cross-country jumps in the next field if you want to try them. Peter – my husband - made them, and Matthew's had a go over them. Go through and help yourselves."

Amber had never done any cross-country jumping before and looked with interest at the homemade jumps spread out around the larger field. There was a tyre jump, a hayrack that looked like a crib and was full of straw, a brush fence encased in a wooden support and a box jump. They all looked so solid and strong and intimidating. You couldn't make any mistakes over these jumps as they wouldn't fall like a show jump.

"Cool," said Emily, looking completely confident as she spurred Honey into an active trot and headed for the tyres. Amber decided to follow suit over the smallest and softest of the jumps, and Pearl amiably hopped over it in Honey's wake. Not sure that she was quite ready to tackle the others yet, Amber pulled Pearl up and watched with surprise as Emily got Honey into a canter and rode strongly for the brush fence. Amber couldn't believe how daring Emily was being on a pony she'd never ridden. A pony that wasn't exactly known for her courage and hadn't done any jumping in her life. She almost couldn't bear to look as Honey neared the fence.

Without even a moment's hesitation, the pony picked up her feathery feet and sailed over the imposing brush fence in one fluid motion. Then, without breaking stride, Emily pushed on to the hayrack and finally finished with the box.

"That was *great*," Emily enthused, her cheeks flushed and her eyes wide. "Has she really not jumped before?"

"No, she hasn't," replied Amber, looking at Honey in a new light. She looked… *different*. It was hard to explain but Honey looked more alive somehow; her face looked bold and happy and she seemed to be throbbing with energy. So much different to the quiet, rather nervous and slightly switched off mare she usually was. "She's jumped a couple of tiny logs in the forestry with Dad, but nothing like that. That was amazing!"

"She's a natural." Emily patted Honey's neck vigorously,

They thanked Mrs Jones, and Amber arranged to ride with Joanne on Saturday before they rode the short distance back to the farm, talking all the way about Honey's remarkable jumping.

When they arrived, they rode by Mrs Anderson's car to see her sitting in the front seat, engrossed in her book. She didn't even look up as their shadow blocked the light across the page she was reading.

"See," said Amber, laughing and rolling her eyes. "I hope you're not dying to get home for your tea. She won't move now until she's finished the chapter."

"Ha, it's just as well I've got two chocolate bars in my bag then isn't it," replied Emily slyly. "Come on, the first person to get untacked gets the one that isn't squashed."

-Five-

Pony for Sale

Friday night saw the members of Blakefield Pony Club arriving at Mrs Best's house for a stable management rally. Amber hadn't been to a stable rally before, but Emily had told her she would need to learn about the correct care and management of horses and ponies if she wanted to do any Pony Club tests. And Amber, determined to have a circle of coloured felt behind her Pony Club badge like everyone else, had decided to start going to the monthly meetings at the DC's house.

Mrs Best's house was old, and stone built. Fairly large and with an impressive entrance of two imposing stone pillars bearing the name 'Linfield,' it looked like it had, in its time, been a grand residence. But now, wrapped tightly in ivy with paint flaking off the walls to reveal previous colours from its long past, the house was an odd contrast of neglect and disrepair, and much-loved family home. Entering the house gave much the same effect. The rooms were large with original features. Much of the furniture was old and probably valuable, but the chairs were threadbare and covered with an assortment of sleeping dogs and cats. Dusty trophies stood tall and proud on the mantelpiece amongst the colourful rosettes that littered every surface, and the walls were full of pictures of different horses and ponies in action, all apparently ridden by the same girl; the photographs chronicling her equestrian pursuits from toddler to adulthood as she beamed happily from the pictures.

The living room was filling up with people who were chatting with each other whilst standing due to the fact there was a cat or dog lounging on every seat in the room. Amber was looking around for familiar faces amongst the members when Mrs Best suddenly exploded into the room.

"Up, up, up, you old lay-a-bouts!" She bustled in, clapping her hands and shrieking loudly so that furry bodies immediately leapt from the sofa and other chairs and scurried to safety.

"Right, parents, there are refreshments in the second sitting room if you'd like to go through," she said, escorting them briskly from the room and shutting the door on them. "Okay then," she turned to look at the people left in the room, "group one, Jean is waiting for you in the feed room. You're doing feeding and nutrition tonight. Off you go then." She waved her arms and the older members trooped off to the feed store.

"Group two, Rachel is in Woody's stable so you can go and see what she has in store for you."

The two girls in the room with Amber (one of whom was Kate from the mounted rally) left, and Amber thought she'd better check which group she was in to avoid making a mistake like she had at her first ridden rally.

"Er… am I in group two?" she asked tentatively as Mrs Best made for the door to join the parents.

"Oh dear! How silly of me, I'd forgotten this was your first one," she bustled. "Yes, group one is for our members aiming at C+ level and above. Your group covers D to C tests. Run and follow Kate and Chelsea, then you'll know where to go."

Amber ran out into the yard and followed Kate and Chelsea into a small barn that held three internal stables with a hayloft above. Standing outside one of the stables was a young woman of nineteen or twenty, dressed in rather holey jeans, wellies, and an oversized checked shirt. And chatting to her were Natalie and Emily.

"Great, you're all here. Let's get started." Rachel put down the tail bandage she had been rolling and went to collect some other items she needed. Amber slipped in between Emily and Natalie, grateful for the company of friends.

"How's Fudge?" she asked Emily. "Any better?"

"The heat and swelling have gone down but he's still not quite right yet."

"Oh." Amber shook her head sadly in sympathy for Emily before turning to Natalie. "And is Sable okay?"

"Well, no. She's totally in the bad books, actually. I was just telling Emily; my dad went to put her in for the night on Tuesday and didn't come back for two hours.

44

Mum and I just thought he'd got talking to someone but eventually, she phoned him to see where he was. He didn't answer so she went to look for him and found him lying flat on his back in the field. Sable had kicked him right in the chest."

"No!" cried Amber, wide-eyed, unable to believe Sable could be that evil. "Is he alright?"

"He's got a cracked rib and he's really bruised. He's off work. Mum had to bring me here tonight. Although…" her voice dropped sadly, "I think I need more than stable management lessons to cope with Sable. I'd be better off learning self-defence! I know she's awful at shows, but I could put up with that if she could just be friendly at least, but she's always horrible to us."

Emily raised an eyebrow and nodded at Amber with a '*see-I-told-you*' look on her face.

***

An hour later, the girls left Woody's stable and traipsed back to the house. Amber and Natalie were aiming at taking their D and D+ tests and had been looking at a grooming kit, identifying the brushes; their names and correct uses. Then they had tacked up a very patient Woody and discussed how to assess a correctly fitting saddle and bridle. The other girls, who were all thirteen and had already passed their D and D+, were preparing for their C test, so Rachel had quizzed them about what to look for in a newly shod hoof, asked them to identify the farrier's tools and describe their uses, and then they each had to rug Woody and put travel boots on while explaining their use.

Amber had really enjoyed the rally and felt she had learned loads as she'd listened in to Emily, Kate and Chelsea while she was putting together a bridle Rachel had given her and Natalie to take apart, clean and reassemble to make sure they knew how it all fitted together.

Back in the house, the dogs and cats had crept unnoticed back onto the chairs while everyone was in the second sitting room. Rachel gently picked up a tightly curled cat, sat down with the cat on her knee and switched on the TV. Amber was surprised at her making herself so at home, when suddenly the faces looking out of the pictures on the walls became familiar and it dawned on her that the girl in the pictures was Rachel. *She must be Mrs Best's daughter*.

"Are these all *your* trophies and rosettes?" Amber asked while Rachel flicked wearily through the channels looking for something to watch.

"Yep," she replied, giving up on the telly and stroking the cat instead, "although there haven't been any new ones for a while. I got most of them on old Woody and another pony I had called Ghost. She was an amazing show-jumper."

Amber looked wistfully at the silverware, thinking that Rachel must be an excellent rider to have amassed such a collection. Rachel caught her expression. "You'll be winning your own trophies soon," she said, encouragingly.

Amber smiled but shook her head. "No, my pony isn't really into competitions. She doesn't like games at all and she's not too fond of jumping either. She is good at handy pony though," she added, not wanting to sound totally negative.

"That's a shame," said Rachel, "I know of a good competition pony that's coming up for sale if you're looking for one. It's won a lot around here. I could give you the number?"

47

"Oh, er, thanks but we're not looking for a new pony," Amber replied hurriedly, thinking that although she would love a jumping pony, she was not prepared to sell Pearl to get one.

***

The next morning the Andersons were all sitting at the kitchen table having breakfast. Their cocker spaniel, Kasper begged beseechingly with his brown, sorrowful eyes and Stig the cat sat in the middle of the tabletop, waiting for the milk from their cereal, trying to mesmerise them into eating faster with his supercilious feline gaze.

"I had a good chat with everyone last night," Mr Anderson started talking, "there's more to the Pony Club than we thought. There are proficiency tests, road safety tests, camp and they do team competitions. There's also area competitions, where you go out of the county to compete against clubs from all over the region." He paused before continuing carefully. "The Pony Club isn't for Pearl, Amber. She doesn't enjoy it and she's not really up to it. Mrs Best was telling me about a pony that's going to be for sale soon, so we thought–"

"No!" Amber interrupted sharply, clattering her spoon into her dish, "I don't want to sell Pearl!"

Mr Anderson smiled, "Who said anything about selling Pearl? If we get another pony it will be *as well* as, not instead of Pearl."

Amber was still suspicious. "Sooo… we'd have *three* ponies?"

"Yes, why not? There's three of us so we'd be able to ride out together."

"We just think you're going to need a better pony to do Pony Club activities," added Amber's mum. "We've got a phone number. Do you want to go and see this pony?"

"*Yeah*!" Amber eagerly agreed, as visions of herself surrounded by red rosettes and silver trophies flashed through her mind.

-Six-

Chalk and Cheese

Mrs Anderson spoke to Mrs Dean, the pony's owner, and it was arranged that they would go and see Molly - the pony – the following Sunday as it was a show-free day. Amber could barely contain her excitement through Saturday and became even more restless to see Molly when Joanne said she knew the pony and confirmed that it had won lots of jumping classes.

"Frankie is a really strong rider though, so you might have to work hard, and make sure you ask them about her back."

"Why, what's wrong with her back?" Mrs Anderson's ears pricked up, riding alongside them. Joanne's mum had only allowed her to go out for a hack with Amber because she knew Mrs Anderson was going with them. She was still worried about her daughter riding out on her new, inexperienced pony even though Merry hadn't put a foot wrong since she'd come to live with them.

"She had an accident at Gosforth show. She was wearing bandages instead of boots and one of the front ones unravelled. She stepped on it with her hind foot right in front of the wall jump and went straight through it. We didn't see them again for a while and we heard she'd hurt her back. After she had time off, she came back and has been jumping since so it's probably fine now, but just watch and see if they mention it," Joanne warned.

"Right," said Amber, her enthusiasm temporarily cooled.

***

Sunday dawned bright and breezy and tingles swept through Amber as they travelled to see the pony. The journey wasn't long, but it seemed like an eternity to Amber until Mrs Anderson finally pulled up outside a terraced house and switched off the engine. She frowned as she checked the address.

"I wonder why they wanted us to meet them here instead of where the pony is kept?" she wondered aloud "Maybe it isn't very far away."

At that moment, the door of the house opened. A tall, lean lady with curly red hair and large square glasses smiled and waved at them from the doorstep.

"Come in, come in!" She ushered them pleasantly from the hall into the living room where Amber saw a collection of trophies and framed photographs to equal Rachel Best's.

"Did Molly win all these trophies?" Amber asked in awe.

"She did indeed. Molly's a very good competition pony. Would you like to see her?"

Mrs Dean smiled down at Amber who nodded distractedly, still taking in the shelves packed with large trophies, shields and smaller silver dishes.

Amber and her mother followed Mrs Dean to the back door, whereupon it was opened to reveal something very unexpected.

"Oh!" gasped Mrs Anderson in surprise.

The back yard of the terraced house was covered in concrete, and on it stood a breezeblock building, a small store and a muckheap. Seemingly unaware of her visitors' surprise at finding out she kept her horses in her back yard, Mrs Dean escorted them into the stone building where they saw two internal stables occupied by horses, and a third that contained mucking out equipment, bales of hay and straw and feed bins. The first stable they came to contained a very large, athletic looking, dark bay thoroughbred.

"That's my endurance horse, Bonfire Bob," explained Mrs Dean. "We've done about ten-thousand miles on endurance rides. He's one tough animal."

They continued to the next stable where a rather stocky girl was grooming a gleaming chestnut pony.

"And this is Molly and my daughter Frankie."

Mrs Dean opened the stable door for Amber to enter. As soon as she was in the stable, the pony turned to look at her. Amber was mesmerised. Her coat was bright chestnut and she had four white socks and a white blaze. She looked like a larger version of Joanne's pony, Flash. Her body was that of an athlete. Long legged, lean and deep chested, Amber knew she would have endless stamina. Strong, bunched muscles showed under the almost metallic coat. This pony was a perfect picture of health and fitness, lightyears away from round, hairy Pearl. They were at different ends of the pony spectrum: like chalk and cheese.

Amber walked nearer to stroke Molly's emblazoned face. The pony regarded her with soft brown eyes, blowing warm air into Amber's hands as she cupped the velvety muzzle and leaned her face against the pony's hard cheek.

"We're very sad to be selling her," Mrs Dean spoke up, "but Fran is too big for her now and she's getting her first horse. She's had a lot of fun with our Molly though, haven't you love?"

Frankie nodded but didn't seem too upset to Amber, who knew that if she had to sell Pearl, she'd be wailing and hanging on to her if anyone came to look at her, to put them off.

"Well, we'd better get her tack on so you can have a try of her then."

Amber went back to the car to get her riding hat, and when she returned, Molly was ready for her. Frankie held her while Amber mounted and adjusted her stirrups. She felt very strange. She hadn't ridden anything but Pearl for such a long time and Molly was a completely different kettle of fish. Pearl was round and short necked with little tiny ears and a thick, bushy mane, whereas Molly was narrow with a long neck lined with a perfectly pulled mane. Her large, pricked ears seemed miles away. Amber felt like she was sitting on a giraffe. Mrs Dean then led Bonfire Bob out and Frankie got on him using the mounting block.

"You can go for a little ride to get used to her first, then you can try her jumping when you get back," Mrs Dean explained. She opened the gate and they walked out into the road, Molly's long walking stride feeling smooth and comfortable.

The ride was all road work so there was nowhere to try a canter, but Molly was very well behaved as she trotted calmly next to the exuberant Bob, who Frankie was having to work very hard to control. Amber found out that the Dean's did not have a field, so the horses were permanently stabled, hence Bob's excitement as he was kept in all day and was so fit, he was ready to burst.

"We have to try and ride him for about three hours a day just to stop him destroying his stable," Frankie told her, "but he's great at endurance. He can do a fifty-mile ride without breaking a sweat. He's like a machine."

Half an hour round the block was obviously not enough to satisfy the big horse, so Frankie guided Amber down a track to where the mothers were waiting and then left again to give him another two hours riding.

At the end of the track was a tiny enclosure of about the size of a twenty-metre circle with a jump made out of a short pole and some crates erected along one side.

"Here we are, dear." Mrs Dean opened the gate for Amber to enter the enclosure. "Have a little pop over that jump and see what you think."

There was no room to trot around first and get settled, so Amber had to go straight for the jump. Molly approached it calmly and hopped over the poles easily.

"Great, hold on!" Mrs Dean tilted the crates which raised the jump to about eighty centimetres. "Try again."

Again, Amber aimed for the jump, in what she now guessed was little more than a chicken enclosure judging by the hen huts beside it, and Molly sailed over it despite the cramped conditions. Amber patted her and rode to the gate.

"So, what do you think?" Mrs Dean asked.

"She's lovely," said Amber, partly because she believed it and partly just to be polite because really, she didn't know what she thought, having only been for a brief ride round the block and tried one jump in such a cramped space.

Mrs Anderson was obviously thinking the same thing as she said, "Thank you for letting us try her but I don't feel we've seen enough to be able to make up our minds. Could we have her on trial for a week to see if they get on?"

Mrs Dean's smile faltered slightly. "Well, I'm afraid that's not possible as somebody else is coming to look at her tomorrow. Molly has a very high reputation around here so I'm sure if you don't want her, they will."

"It's not that we don't want her, and I'm aware she's a very good pony, its just…"

"I'm sorry, Mrs Anderson but if you want her, you'll have to decide today as the people coming tomorrow are from our own Pony Club and know her well. They're very keen to have her."

Mrs Anderson paused for a minute, not knowing what to say. She was not entirely happy with being rushed into a decision, but on the other hand, the pony came highly recommended, and it was probably true that they would miss out on it if she didn't decide today.

"I'll tell you what," she said, "I'll agree to buy Molly if you can cancel tomorrow's viewers so I can have her vetted. I'll give you a deposit now and if she passes the vet, I'll pay the rest. If she fails, you can keep the deposit and you'll still have the pony to sell."

Mrs Dean looked undecided for a moment, but realising she couldn't lose anything out the deal being offered, she agreed.

-Seven-

Just Molly

As Amber stared at the ticking clock at school the following Monday, she realised that time really does go slower when you're waiting for something. She had spent all day impatiently drumming her fingernails against the table, unable to concentrate on any lesson as she daydreamed about show jumping Molly over enormous fences and beating Elisha. Yes, that was what she most hoped to achieve: to put Elisha in her place – *second* place. But Amber was getting ahead of herself. Everything depended on Molly passing the vet's examination that was taking place at 4pm that day. Only if she were given a clean bill of health would she belong to Amber.

The last lesson of the day was geography, a class Amber usually enjoyed as Miss Lewis was her favourite teacher and she was able to sit with her best (although totally un-horsey) friend, Sarah. But today she could hardly keep herself in her seat and was so totally unable to disguise her restlessness that she received some very puzzled looks from Miss Lewis, who was used to Amber being completely attentive in her lessons.

When the bell went to signal the end of the day, it was like the trigger of a rocket launch. Without waiting to walk out with Sarah as she always did, Amber leapt off her chair and ran from the room, calling back to a rather peeved looking Sarah, "Sorry, I've really got to go. See you tomorrow!"

And with that she raced through the corridors, squeezing through gaps between students who were making their way out annoyingly slowly, and across the netball courts to the queue of parents in their cars.

By the time Amber wrenched open her own car door and flung herself into the passenger seat as if she were making a quick getaway from a bank robbery, she was quite out of breath. She sat, puffing and red as a pillar box while Mrs Anderson laughed at her daughter's sudden appearance.

"Look at you, breaking the speed limit! What's the emergency?"

Amber looked crossly at her mother, "You know what. We're going to get Molly vetted, aren't we?"

"Yes, we are, but I don't know why you've rushed down here and left Sarah behind as if your life depended on it. We're going to be sitting in this traffic for at least ten minutes before we can even move."

Sure enough, Mrs Anderson was right as it took precisely twelve minutes (Amber was counting) before the cars and buses started to filter slowly out of the school gates. Much to Amber's embarrassment, Sarah had, just a few minutes after Amber, climbed into her car, which was parked three ahead of Amber's and had left the school first.

***

The vet was already waiting in the Dean's backyard when Amber and her mother arrived. Amber felt a flutter in her stomach when she saw Molly, the light dancing on her perfectly smooth, red coat as Frankie held her for the vet.

"Right, let's take a look," the vet proclaimed, flourishing a stethoscope from his pocket and placing it on Molly's side.

Amber watched anxiously as the vet, a tall man with large, strong hands, examined Molly thoroughly. He listened to her heart and breathing and felt along her limbs, back, neck and pelvis in the yard, then they went out into the alley and Molly was trotted up and down before having various flexion tests performed and finally, her heart and breathing were checked again.

"Well," the vet began, zipping up his bag and slinging it over his shoulder before delivering his verdict, "this is a very fit, healthy pony. She has an excellent heartbeat and her wind is fine. I believe she's had an injury to her back?" he enquired, looking at Mrs Dean.

"Yes, two years ago, but it healed well, and she's had no trouble since."

"Well, it's up to you," he turned to Mrs Anderson. "She's a fit mare and as sound as a pound. I can't detect any problems with her back, but backs are funny things. It could go again in the future, or on the other hand, it might not. It depends whether you want to take the risk."

With that, he shook hands with the two women and left, leaving Mrs Anderson to make up her mind. Thinking it over, she considered that although Molly could have a problem with her back later on, the vet had said it was fine at the moment and that in all other ways she was exceptionally fit and healthy. She also knew that Amber was a small, lightweight rider who wouldn't put undue pressure on Molly's back by being too heavy for her. She looked at Frankie, who was much heavier than Amber and decided that, compared to her, Molly wouldn't even feel her daughter's weight. Plus, there was always the chance that she was completely healed, and the problem would never return.

"What do you want to do then?" Asked Mrs Dean, not unpleasantly.

"Well, I'm satisfied with the vet's verdict, so I think I owe you some more money."

Amber suddenly realised she'd been holding her breath waiting for her mother's decision and gasped loudly when she heard what she'd been desperately hoping for. She felt so happy she could burst.

Everyone was all smiles except for Frankie. Amber noticed the girl's reaction to the news was not as gleeful as everyone else's. Her eyes were flat and expressionless as she raised a hand to stroke Molly's nose. Her face gave nothing away, but Amber could tell from her slumped shoulders and the tender way she stroked the pony that she was not happy.

Seeing Frankie's sadness made Amber's bubbling excitement settle to a simmer, as she knew Molly would soon belong to her, but she could imagine how awful this must feel to the girl who was losing her pony.

Following Frankie when she turned to take Molly back to her stable, she ventured uncertainly, "I know this must be horrible for you, but she'll have a good home. She'll have plenty of company and will be able to go out in the field with our ponies. We'll take good care of her, and you'll probably still see her at shows."

"I know, I'm not upset really," Frankie opened the stable door and led Molly inside, "once she goes, we can bring my new horse home and I'm looking forward to that. It's just that I'll miss her. She's been a good pony."

Amber felt slightly awkward and cast around for something else to say. "So, is there anything else I should know about her?"

They began walking back to the house.

"Only that she doesn't like having rugs put on or having her girth done up. She gnashes but we never tie her up and she's never bitten anyone."

"What do you mean, she gnashes?"

"Oh, she pulls faces and snaps her teeth together, but she doesn't bite. She just likes to let you know she's not impressed!"

"Oh, right!"

The two mothers were both smiling and talking happily, waiting by the front door when Amber and Frankie got back to the house.

"Come on then," Mrs Anderson beckoned to Amber, "let's go and get our tea. Thanks again," she shook Mrs Dean's hand, "and we'll see you at the weekend."

Saturday morning was like Christmas to Amber. She was so excited she couldn't sleep, so she got up at 6am and tried to keep busy while she waited for it to be time to go to the farm. Molly was being delivered at 10am.

Eventually, after tidying her room, feeding Stig and Kasper, cleaning out the goldfish, flicking through a magazine and having breakfast, it was finally time to set off. Mr Anderson was as keen to see Molly as Amber, as he'd been at work during the trial and the vetting and so hadn't even seen his daughter's new pony yet. He kept calling her 'Good Golly Miss Molly,' which Amber found irritating. It was a song from the olden days apparently.

They arrived in plenty of time to get Molly's stable ready. Hers was an enormous loose box right next to the farmer's daughter's horse, Oriel. The big bay mare was already looking out of her top door, seemingly aware that something was going on due to all the hustle and bustle going on around her. Honey and Pearl didn't have a clue what was going on, however, as their large shared stable and yard were around the corner and out of sight.

The stable for Molly hadn't had a horse in it for some time and had been used to store old furniture, bits of machinery and so on. But when Mrs Anderson had asked Jerry the farmer if it would be possible to bring another pony, he had been excellent. He and his sons, fifteen-year-old Daniel and eighteen-year-old Jack had cleared the stable of all its contents and cleaned away all the dust and cobwebs, then his daughter, Caroline had whitewashed all the walls until it looked like a brand new stable. And now, with its hay bracket full and deep straw bed neatly arranged, it was ready for its new occupant.

***

On the dot of 10am, the Dean family rolled up the dusty farm track and into the yard. The front ramp of the trailer was lowered, and Molly's striking face poked out, her nostrils dilated and quivering and her eyes wide and worried as she was led down the ramp into the unfamiliar place. Frankie took her straight into her new stable and removed her rug, bandages and head collar.

Molly instantly began exploring the strange new area sniffing and breathing deeply at the fresh new straw, the walls, and the hay. Then, as if she knew what was happening, she ran to the stable door and flung her head out, whinnying loudly to the Deans, who were walking back to the car. Amber's heart went out to her. *She* knew Molly would be getting well looked after and loved here, but to the pony, it must seem like being abandoned to an uncertain future with strange, new people.

"Enjoy her Amber," said Mrs Dean, who looked a bit teary. "Make sure you win everything on her. She's got her reputation to keep up," she joked weakly.

"Does she have a show name?" Asked Amber, knowing that her dad would be itching to call her that annoying song title he kept singing.

"We couldn't think of anything spectacular or imaginative when we got her so she's simply 'Just Molly'. It suits her – she's so good she doesn't need a fancy name."

With that, the Deans climbed back into their car and drove away.

The Andersons stood and looked at each other. Mrs Anderson was the one to break the silence. "Well, we've got a pony, but nothing for her. If you're going to ride her, we'd better sort some tack out."

When they'd bought the Fell ponies, Claire had helpfully included their tack in the sale, but this hadn't been the case with Molly.

"Let's go down and see if Claire has any tack we can borrow until we get sorted," suggested Mr Anderson.

***

Claire had been very helpful and given them a simple snaffle bridle and several saddles to try.

"They might be a bit wide for her," she said, loading the third saddle into the car, as most of Claire's horses and ponies were natives and cobs, "but the last one is probably your best bet. It was Rosie's – a fairly slim pony I used to have. They're all for sale anyway, so if you want any of them just let me know."

The following day, with Caroline's help, they tried the saddles on Molly. Caroline was very quiet and gentle but obviously very knowledgeable as she inserted her fingers between the saddle and Molly's back, peered down the gullet and pulled at the cantle. Just as Claire had predicted, Caroline rejected the first two saddles as they were too wide and would put pressure on Molly's spine and withers, but the third met with her approval.

"This one seems okay," she said quietly as she repeated the assessment methods, "it's a narrower fit so it isn't pressing on her spine and there's plenty of clearance here." She showed them the four-finger gap between the withers and the pommel. "I'll have to see what it's like with you sitting on it," she told Amber.

Mrs Anderson produced one of Honey's girths and fastened it to the saddle. Frankie's warning proved true: as the girth was tightened, Molly put her ears back and started snapping her teeth, but she never turned her head to bite and she was soon tacked up and ready to go.

Amber mounted and Caroline checked the saddle again before watching as they walked and did a little trot around the yard.

"It seems a good fit," she told Amber's parents, "it doesn't restrict Molly's movement and it's the right size for Amber too. A nice quality saddle."

Mr Anderson thanked Caroline, who blushed and muttered that it was nothing, and Amber was left sitting in the yard on Molly.

"Well, I guess we'll go and get Honey and Pearl and ride out with you," said Mr Anderson, "why don't you go down and show Molly to Joanne while you're waiting?"

***

There was no-one around when Amber arrived at Jubilee House, so she dismounted and opened the gate before leading Molly to the front door and ringing the bell. When Joanne opened the door, her eyes nearly popped out of her head as she saw Amber standing there holding Molly.

"Oh wow, you got her!" She came straight out and started looking Molly up and down. "Isn't there a show on at Brantfort Bridge today? I thought you'd have been going."

"We only got her yesterday," Amber explained, "and she didn't have any tack. We've had to borrow some off Claire. We're just letting her settle in first before we go anywhere. And I need to get used to her too. We're all going for a ride now; I'm just waiting for them to come down."

"Oooo, come and do some jumps in the field until they get here," said Joanne excitedly, "let's see what she's like."

***

Amber felt rather nervous about jumping Molly in front of Joanne, who obviously had such high expectations, especially as she'd only jumped her over a small fence in a very enclosed space on her trial. Nerves were soon replaced with elation, however, as Molly cleared the jumps in the paddock effortlessly. There was no pulling or charging, just smooth, controlled jumping from a pony that was completely willing. Amber had never felt anything like it. Jumping on Molly was like floating. Joanne was all for putting the jumps up higher when Amber's parents arrived to meet her.

"Call for me after school next week, I'll ride out with you," called Joanne as Amber rode away with her parents.

"Yeah," she replied distantly, looking down at the unfamiliar chestnut mane in front of her.

Amber was in heaven. Molly was the best pony she could ever have wished for.

- Eight -

Speed Demon

"I hope you don't mind but Matthew's coming with us," said Joanne glumly as Amber arrived at her house with Molly. "Mum says he's got to come because Dad's at work and she needs to go shopping and Matthew whinges something awful if he has to go shopping. Sorry." She rolled her eyes in apology that her little brother would be accompanying them.

Amber laughed at Joanne's exasperation at having to look after her brother and wondered fleetingly what it would be like to have brothers and sisters.

"Don't worry, it's fine if Matthew comes. I don't mind!"

Joanne's younger brother was a quiet boy with dark curly hair and freckles, quite the opposite of Joanne with her pale skin and straight blonde hair. He rode Sam, a lovely hairy bay pony with a bushy black mane and tail and feathery feet. Amber knew Matthew wouldn't trouble them on the ride, he would just plod away at the back in silence thinking about whatever nine-year-old boys think about, while she and his sister rode together at the front chatting non-stop all the way round.

"Isn't your mum or dad coming with us?" Joanne asked, seeing that Amber was on her own.

"Not this time. Dad's brought me today but Honey has lost a shoe so he can't ride: Pearl's too small for him, so it's just me."

"Oh well, we'll be fine. Mum seems to think I need a babysitter. What does she think is going to happen? Merry's an angel compared to Flash and I hardly think Sam is going to have a psychotic moment. We'll just have a nice quiet ride out and she needn't even know we went on our own."

Molly and Merry matched each other perfectly, both being the same size and build with the same length of stride. Amber couldn't wait to get back to the forestry hill so they could race up it and see who was the fastest. When she'd ridden with her parents on Sunday, they'd just walked and trotted, so she couldn't wait to have a gallop. Racing would be a whole new experience for Amber as riding with Joanne had always previously meant her getting left behind on Pearl while Flash sped away on his own. Now they had ponies that were much more equally matched, things would be a lot more interesting.

"Do you want to canter here?" Joanne asked as they'd reached the short uphill part of the narrow track they were riding single file on, where they usually cantered. The path didn't last very long before it became rocky and began winding down into the valley, but it was a nice place to have a short, gentle canter before they had to walk to the bottom.

"Yeah great," she replied from her position behind Joanne and Merry and gathered up her reins to set off.

Molly was not used to this sort of riding; her previous outings had either been competing at shows or being ridden on the roads. The feel of soft earth beneath her feet and the sight of Merry cantering away in front of her was just too much excitement for her to bear. The pony couldn't stay calm and controllable when she could feel all her energy bubbling through her body, her rider was so light she could hardly feel her, there were other ponies to race and she had this lovely straight track to run on.

Amber felt the rush of energy surge beneath her as Molly launched into a gallop. She felt no joy or exhilaration from the tremendous speed of her mount as they gained quickly on Merry, only terror as she heaved on the reins to no avail. Instead of slowing down, Molly was pulling against her and her speed was building.

"AAAAAAARGHHHHHHH!" she screamed as they were nearly upon Joanne.

Joanne turned just in time to see Molly drawing up against Merry's quarters and acting instinctively, she pulled Merry back to allow Molly past before she pushed them off the track. The palomino obediently responded and slowed to a trot as Molly streaked past like a thoroughbred racehorse.

"What happened?" demanded Joanne incredulously as Matthew caught up on Sam.

"Dunno, she just went – like Flash, nought to sixty in one second!"

"Oh no," she moaned, "come on. We'll have to try and catch her."

With that, she urged Merry into a trot. Despite the urgency of the situation, there was no way she was risking cantering down the rocky downhill path, never mind galloping.

Meanwhile, a thoroughly terrified Amber was still hurtling along ahead at an unbelievable speed considering the terrain. Tears streamed down her face and blurred her vision and her bare hands were raw from pulling the reins. Wild with fright, she frantically racked her brain for ideas, now having to lean forward to avoid being thrashed by low hanging branches. Feeling her rider leaning higher up her neck, Molly surged forward with even greater speed. Suddenly Amber remembered how Elisha had stopped Rocky from his bolt by turning him in circles.

But the path is too narrow! her brain screamed in despair.

She tried hauling on one rein, then the other rather than pulling both at once. This had the effect of turning Molly's head slightly to the side, but being much stronger than her rider, the pony was easily able to wrench the taut, restricting rein away.

Amber sobbed with fear and frustration. The path had become flat again and Molly levelled out, her long legs stretching ahead of her as she reached blistering speeds. In a few more strides Amber knew they would come to a fork in the path. She needed to take a sharp turn to the right, almost doubling back on herself to get up onto a higher forestry track. The path that went straight ahead led out to the road.

She could see through her tears, not far ahead were the old stone gateposts where the path divided. She began pulling the right rein with all her might to try and get Molly to turn onto the uphill path where she hoped she could stop her. But to make the acute turn, Molly would have to slow down or risk falling, and she had already spied the straight path ahead of her. Deciding she would much rather continue galloping straight on than slow down and make a turn, the pony seized the bit and resisted Amber's concerted efforts to pull her round, charged through the old gate posts and sped along the path ahead.

Amber's brain screamed at her the urgency of the need to stop before they reached the road, but she could fight no longer. The skin on her hands was torn and blistered, her legs had turned to jelly, and her breath came in painful gasps between sobs. She was exhausted. Knowing that she had no chance of stopping Molly before the road, she contemplated throwing herself off into the hedgerow. But even as the thought occurred to her, she knew she couldn't do it – she was too frightened to move – so she sat there feeling the mighty muscles beneath her as Molly powered on, not tiring in the slightest, the fear inside her reaching breaking point.

"HELP!" she screamed in desperation, "HELP, HELP, HELP!"

As if in answer, there was a loud rumble and a tractor pulled out of a field beside the lane, completely blocking the path. Molly saw it and immediately checked her speed, sliding to a bumpy halt in front of the tractor and shooting Amber out of the saddle and up her neck where she remained, slumped and sobbing with relief that the ordeal was finally over. The farmer, now recovered from the temporary shock of seeing an out of control pony hurtling towards his tractor, climbed out and took hold of the reins. Far from being tired from the exertion, Molly was feeling positively invigorated from the experience. Her eyes were shining, and she champed the bit in annoyance at being stopped before she was ready, but she allowed the farmer to hold her and stood still while he turned his attention to the girl who was shaking and crying uncontrollably on its back.

"Now then lass," he spoke kindly, "tis over now. Yer alright. Come on, sit up, I've got yer."

Still trembling, Amber pushed herself back up Molly's neck and sat back in the saddle, wiping her swollen, red eyes. She looked down at her rescuer. Far from being a tall, handsome hero, the farmer looked at least sixty and wasn't an inch over 5ft 3. He was a startling old man to look at, being so small, but with big muscular arms and hands like spades. His face was brown and crinkly with piercing bright blue eyes and his white wispy hair was standing on end as if he had just pulled a hat off his head.

"Tis a fine spirited pony you've got 'ere lass," he remarked, sweeping his eyes over Molly's athletic frame. "A right la'al thoroughbred."

"She's just bolted with me," Amber explained breathlessly as she made to dismount.

"Whoa there, lass!" exclaimed the old man, putting up a hand to signal Amber to stay put. "You don't wanna be gittin off! You git off now, you'll never git back on. You need to master her. Best cure for a bolter is to tek it, get it garn and then, when it wants to stop, keep it garn till it can't ga ne more. That'll make the beast think!" He smiled a toothy grin revealing a large gap in his smile.

"Oh no," replied Amber with a mixture of horror and resignation, "that won't work with her. She doesn't stop – she goes on forever." She thought with a sickening lurch in her stomach of the never-ending gallop through the forest.

"Ah, they can't ga on foriver lass. They's not machines." He shook his head sagely.

Just then there was a clatter on the cobbled path and Joanne and Matthew appeared looking flustered with twigs and pine needles sticking out of their hats and hair. Amber was touched to see that Joanne's face was creased with concern, but on seeing Amber was safe and sound, relief washed away the worry and she seemed to sag as if a weight had been lifted off her.

"Oh, thank God you're okay!" she cried. "We were so worried. Now I know what it must've been like for you last year when Elisha and I disappeared. Oh hi, Mr Greeves," she addressed the farmer who was still holding Molly.

"Hallo, lass," he replied heartily, then looked up at Amber with his bright blue eyes twinkling out of his nut-brown face. "Remember what I said lass. You'll 'ave to get the better of her or you'll always be afeared. You should turn around and give her a stinkin' good gallop back up the hill till she's on her knees. Cure her for sure."

Amber smiled weakly and gathered up the reins in her raw, tender hands. "Thanks for your help, but I just can't. I'm going to walk back along the road."

Mr Greeves let go of Molly and gave her a vigorous pat before shrugging his shoulders and climbing back into his tractor.

- Nine -

The Good, the Bad and the Unexpected

Amber was full of trepidation as she sat in the car on the way to her first competition with Molly. After Mr Greeves had driven away in his tractor, the three of them had ridden all the way back along the road at a walk as Amber was so worried Molly would bolt again. Molly, on the other hand, had no intention of galloping off. As soon as she felt the familiar tarmac under her hooves, something in her brain switched off and she ambled home like a perfectly docile donkey.

Later in the week, she'd ridden with her parents – she went back onto Pearl while her mum rode Molly in case she misbehaved. But, as if she wanted to make a liar of Amber, Molly was perfectly good and even enjoyed a quiet canter. Amber was now sure her parents thought she had exaggerated her recount of the ride with Joanne and Matthew and that she was overreacting – Molly hadn't bolted with her – she was just much faster than Pearl, and Amber would soon get used to her.

Amber wasn't so sure. She'd been so happy when Molly was bought for her but now...

Molly had made her feel fear. Amber had *never* felt afraid riding Pearl or any of the ponies in the riding school, but now she knew what it was like to be scared of an animal's strength. And she hated that feeling. She thought forward to her show jumping later in the afternoon. All images of herself leading the lap of honour, waving her red rosette while Elisha trailed behind her in second place had vanished, to be replaced with pictures of Molly careering wildly around the arena with herself just trying to hang on. She closed her eyes and groaned softly. Molly had such a high reputation in competitions; if Amber didn't do well, she knew what people would say. It would be all her fault. The pressure made Amber's stomach turn over. She wondered if you could be physically sick from worrying.

"Are you okay Amber? You look rather green."

Amber was not alone in the back of the car. Emily sat with her. The vet had proclaimed Fudge was sound again but had advised that he only do gentle work for the next few weeks as Pony Club camp was coming up and light work would ensure he would be okay to go. When Emily had relayed the news to Amber at the last stable management rally and gloomily told her Fudge wasn't allowed to do the fun-jump at the weekend, Amber had asked her dad if they could take Honey for Emily to ride, remembering how well she'd gone for Emily in Joanne's field.

And so, Emily had brought her riding gear and stayed the night. Now they were off to Blakefield's fun-jump with Molly and Honey in the trailer behind.

They arrived early, before any of the classes had even begun, but already the field was filling up with rows of trailers and lorries, their colourful metallic paint gleaming in the sunlight. They unloaded the ponies and Amber noted with interest their different reactions to their new surroundings. Molly surveyed the scene hopefully but seemed to look disappointed and bored as she was tied up. Honey on the other hand, who had never travelled in the trailer or been to a show before, stood at the top of the ramp looking around cautiously, her ears pricked so that they nearly touched – her eyes wide and nostrils flared. She looked like she was having a very serious think about whether she was going to venture out of the trailer or not. Eventually, after being coaxed and cajoled with a large carrot, she allowed herself to be led down the ramp and tied up next to Molly. The girls left Amber's parents with the ponies while they went off to place their entries.

The schedule pinned to the caravan window showed that there were five classes starting at sixty centimetres and ending with a metre. In a change since last year, the classes were no longer linked to the size of the pony. Now, any size of horse or pony could be entered in any height class to make allowances for the different levels of ability and experience.

"What are you going to enter?" Amber asked Emily while nervously deciding what she herself should enter. When she was on Pearl, the decision was made for her as Pearl could only really manage the first two classes, but nobody would be expecting her to enter the little classes with Molly. Her stomach did a backflip and took a bow, celebrating its acrobatic skills.

"Well, it says you can enter two height classes," answered Emily, following the writing with a finger and pursing her lips as she thought. "I think I'll do the first two heights as it's only Honey's first show." And with that, she stepped up into the caravan to place her entries, leaving Amber still fretting outside.

After much deliberation, Amber, at last, decided that she could get away with saying she was still getting used to Molly, it was almost the first time she'd jumped on her, and therefore not feel too much of a wimp for not entering the highest classes. She left the caravan with Emily, both carrying their numbers, having entered the seventy and eighty centimetre classes and feeling slightly happier. Although she still felt as if worms were wriggling and writhing in her stomach, the overpowering urge to be sick had lessened.

***

Emily looked very smart on Honey as they warmed up for the first class. Honey's eyes were still popping as she took in the sights and sounds of the show field, but Emily remained calm – oblivious to Honey's shies and spooks - and soon the pony settled, drawing confidence from her rider as they jumped the practice fence, just as she had when Emily rode her in Joanne's field.

As she was watching Honey canter serenely towards the practice fence, Amber heard a "hi!" behind her. She turned to see Natalie, who had ridden over on Sable to begin warming up.

"Aren't you in this class?" she asked Amber.

"No, I'm in the next two. I've brought my new pony, Molly, today."

"Oh. Can't wait to see her."

"I'm just watching Emily. She's riding our Honey and she's never been to a show before. Fudge is still on light duties until camp so we said Emily could borrow Honey for the fun-jump."

"Ah." Natalie's eyes found the black Fell pony and followed its progress over the practice jump. "Well, I'd better warm-up. I'm in this class and they're ready to start."

"Good luck!" called Amber as Natalie rode away and the first competitor was called to enter the ring.

There were lots of competitors in the class and most people were going clear. Emily was near the end of the class so Amber changed into her riding clothes and rode around on Molly for a while. She was sitting on her, at the ringside, flanked by both parents when Emily was announced.

"Emily Pryde, riding Townend Honeysuckle!" They hadn't had to think of a show name for Honey; as she was a registered Fell pony, she already had a name.

The whistle blew and the speakers crackled. Honey jumped and her ears twitched back. Amber could see Emily's lips moving and knew she was talking gently to reassure the startled pony. Emily nudged Honey into a canter and proceeded smoothly to the first fence.

The round must have only lasted a minute as Honey cantered around, her long, bushy black tail billowing out behind her, happily jumping fences as if she was a pro. They gave a loud cheer as she jumped the last fence to gain a clear round.

"Honey's first ever class and she's in the jump-off," cried Mrs Anderson incredulously, Who would've thought it?"

They watched the remaining three competitors, and saw the first two go clear, only to be followed by another disastrous round from Natalie and Sable. As it was a fun-jump and Natalie was last to go in the class, they were a bit more relaxed with the rules and allowed Natalie to continue after she'd got two refusals by the second fence. However, as Sable continued to stop at every jump and parents waiting for the jump-off started shooting accusatory looks at Mr Best, he had to ask Natalie to leave the arena.

Honey went just as well in the jump-off. Emily didn't push her or make her do tight turns, as she knew the pony had never competed before, but Honey looked as though she was thoroughly enjoying herself.

As there had been so many in the class, Emily and Honey weren't placed but nevertheless, everyone was delighted with their performance – none more so than Honey herself, it seemed. The shy, timid pony Amber knew had disappeared. Her eyes shone and she arched her neck regally, as if inviting people to admire her.

The next class also had a lot of entries and Amber could feel herself getting in a knot as she felt more and more nervous waiting for her turn. Molly had warmed up quietly and was showing no signs of doing anything naughty, but still Amber felt like something large and prickly had got stuck in her throat.

"Next into the arena is Emily Pryde and Townend Honeysuckle. Stand by Amber Anderson and Just Molly," came Mr Best's voice over the tannoy.

Hearing her name called sent Amber into her own little bubble. Sounds became muffled and her vision became hazy as she stared out in front of her but saw nothing. The next thing she knew, her name was being called again over the loudspeaker. Emily had already left the arena and Amber had seen nothing of her round. Feeling a mixture of guilt, nerves and anticipation, she rode into the arena and cantered at the sound of the whistle.

Molly's canter was smooth, balanced and effortless. She approached the first fence and was over it without Amber even feeling anything – it was just like another canter stride. They floated around the rest of the course gliding comfortably over the fences so easily it was like they weren't there. As they cantered out of the arena amidst gentle applause and "*that's a clear round!*" ringing in her ears, Amber's shoulders slumped, and she had to lean her hands on Molly's withers to support her weight; she was weak with relief and happiness. She patted Molly gratefully as Emily and Natalie came to congratulate her; Emily still mounted on Honey, Natalie now on foot.

"Well done Amber! That means we're against each other in the jump-off now," grinned Emily.

"She went lovely didn't she?" Natalie stroked Molly's blaze, a mournful look on her face. "I wish I had a pony like her, one that would just jump without a fuss. Sable totally hates competing."

"Why don't you sell her and get a pony that's more …agreeable?" suggested Emily, choosing her words carefully.

Natalie sighed deeply. "I'd love to, but who'd buy her?"

"Not everybody wants a pony for jumping. Plenty of people just want to hack out. Is she a nice ride?"

"Yeah, she's quite nice but she's so grumpy and bad-tempered, she'd put people off. Who wants a pony that can't even be nice?" Natalie shrugged her shoulders and looked thoroughly fed up. Amber was about to repeat what Emily had once told her, about horses and people either getting on or making each other miserable, but bit her lip and decided to keep it to herself. She didn't think Natalie would be too pleased to hear that it might be her making her pony miserable and that Sable might be much happier and less bad-tempered with someone else.

By this time the remaining competitors had completed their rounds and the order for the jump-off was being called.

Amber didn't have much experience of jump-off technique, not having been in any, but she'd watched enough of them to pick up some tips. She silently memorised the new shortened course and planned her route – where she could save time by cutting corners or going inside fences – and where she could push Molly on.

The first few competitors went quite well, but none of them had taken Amber's planned short cut inside number six; they'd all gone around. When her name was called,

93

Amber entered the arena suddenly unsure of the route she would take – *Should I stick to my plan, or be careful and take the long route?*

Once again Molly loped forward into a smooth canter. They cleared the first and Amber pushed on to the next fence. Molly immediately lengthened her stride and stood off the second jump, but was still perfectly under control. They cleared the wall and Molly was going so well, Amber decided to cut inside fence six as she had planned and jump the double from two strides. Molly responded instantly to her aids and popped over the double easily.

As she brought Molly back to a trot, patting her furiously, she heard her time over the loudspeaker. She was the quickest yet. She was in the lead!

"Well done, that was brilliant! Well ridden!" Emily cheered generously as she rode past Amber into the arena.

"Thanks," gasped Amber. "Good luck."

After Amber, many of the remaining competitors copied her turn inside number six, but one after another, as their times were read out, Amber remained in the lead. Growing more and more excited that she was about to achieve her ambition and win a jumping class, she held her breath as the last rider started his round. Fiercely competitive, he charged over the fences, kicking madly in between the spread-out ones and yanking sharply at his pony's bit on the turns. He too turned inside to the last fence – the double – but pulled his pony around so roughly the poor thing momentarily lost its footing. Gamely, it still tried to jump but the stride wasn't right, and the top pole came down. When the time was announced, he was the fastest and would've won if he hadn't had the double down. Amber felt sorry for the boy's pony as he rode out with a face like thunder – it had tried its best for him, despite his rather rough riding and the boy obviously didn't appreciate it – but soon a great swell of joy was rising in her as the results were called. She was the winner and Honey had come in sixth place after gaining another clear in her jump-off. Amber had never felt so elated as she led the lap of honour around the arena, her red rosette fluttering in the breeze on Molly's bridle. She was dimly aware of people clapping around her, but she couldn't take it in. It was like being back in one of her dreams. She had won her first ever class and it was the best feeling in the world. She never wanted it to end.

Amber had never seen her parents so excited. They were full of congratulations for Amber and gave Molly nearly half a packet of Polo mints, which she crunched up loudly before searching for more. The other half of the packet, unfortunately for Molly, was being fed lovingly to Honey, whom everyone was absolutely delighted with.

"Thanks for letting me ride her," Emily thanked Amber's parents while fondly smoothing Honey's long forelock, "she was great, and I really enjoyed it."

"Oh, no problem," cried Mrs Anderson. "It's been a pleasure and a surprise to see her doing so well. Thank you!"

Amber felt much more confident as she rode into the arena for her next round. She couldn't wait to get started and feel Molly's wonderful jump again. A gate had been added and many of the jumps now had colourful fillers placed under the poles. Amber felt a thrill of excitement as she rode purposefully for the first fence.

As with the first round, Molly jumped carefully and easily, her experience showing as she took the gate and coloured fillers without a second glance. Amber concentrated hard on remembering the course and riding

Molly as well as she could. Soon it was all over. Another clear round.

She didn't have as long to wait for the jump-off in this class as fewer people managed to get clear rounds. One of the fillers displaying a vivid orange and black tiger's face was causing problems and several ponies refused to go over. The jump-off course was soon ready, and Amber felt her insides flutter again as she surveyed the jumps, now standing at eighty-five centimetres and looking positively monumental.

"You can do it. Molly can do it. Don't be nervous." she told herself firmly, breathing in deep, calming breaths.

Once again, she watched others tackle the course before her, some attempting the tight turn to the double, others playing safe and going around. By the time it was her turn there hadn't been any fast clears, so Amber resolved to do her best to win again.

Molly responded well to her new, more urgent riding and cleared the fences well until only the double remained. The double was now bigger with fillers under the first part and a back pole added to the second. As Amber steered Molly round to cut inside, she gave her an extra little kick to give her the impulsion she would need to clear the bigger jumps.

It didn't work.

Just as Amber was getting ready to lean forward and move her hands up Molly's neck for the take-off, Molly pulled up and stopped right in front of the fence. Momentarily shocked that Molly had refused, Amber quickly composed herself and brought Molly round for a second and final attempt, giving her plenty of space to approach now that her chance of winning had gone. Amber could feel herself growing hot as she knew many pairs of eyes were watching her, many of whom belonged to people who knew Molly. They would be tutting and shaking their heads.

She rode strongly, determined not to be eliminated. Molly jumped in over the first part unenthusiastically and was backing off the second part as soon as she landed. Amber brandished her whip and smacked Molly on the shoulder, willing her to jump. Much to her surprise, the pony went straight up in the air in an awkward cat jump. She didn't stretch for the spread at all and brought the whole fence crashing down underneath her. The team of helpers rushed to rebuild the fence again while a shamefaced Amber left the arena.

What happened? What caused Molly to go from the winner of one class to almost being eliminated in the next? Was it me? Have I ruined her already, is that possible? What will my parents say? Amber's mind was so full of thoughts, she didn't even notice the blue and yellow horsebox she was riding past or the loud "hello," as she went by.

"Amber!"

Amber's head snapped up and her brain was wrenched away from its thoughts as she heard her name being called. Her mood dropped even further when she saw who it was that had addressed her. Elisha was in the process of putting a saddle on her black horse. She finished pulling the girth up and ducked under his neck, walking directly up to Amber.

Amber leant away from Elisha's approach, like a flower bowing to a storm.

"New pony." It was a statement, not a question. "That's Frankie Dean's' Molly isn't it?" Elisha said, tilting her head slightly.

"Yeah." Then she wished she'd said no, actually, it was *her* Molly.

Elisha's mouth curled into a little smile as she detected the tone in Amber's voice.

"She's a really good jumper – won loads with Frankie. She'll be a big change for you after riding that fat little Fell pony. It's about time you got something decent and started taking competitions seriously."

Amber felt her temper rising but she didn't reply. She didn't want to give Elisha the satisfaction of upsetting her again.

"You'll be going in the big classes today then?" Elisha asked, pushing Amber further.

"No, I've just finished actually," Amber retorted curtly, trying to ride away from Elisha before she said anything else. As she went to steer Molly around her, Elisha caught hold of the pony's reins and began stroking her nose while she looked up at Amber with her hard, blue eyes.

"You've been in the little classes?" she gasped. "What an insult to Molly! You're not riding your no-hope Fell pony anymore. What's the point having a beauty like Molly

100

if you're just going to do the baby classes? She's too good for that."

"I…I'm still getting used to her and I'm not used to big jumps and…and we won our first class so…" Amber flustered until Elisha interrupted.

"Oh, you won a seventy centimetre class? Well done, you'll be at the Olympics next. And how did you do in the other class?"

Amber stared at Elisha, who stared right back, that annoying smirk still playing at the corners of her lips. Amber wilted under the force of Elisha's piercing gaze and broke eye contact.

"Get lost, Elisha!" Amber kicked Molly on so that Elisha had to drop the reins and step aside to avoid being trodden on.

"Ooooh, touchy!" Elisha called to Amber's retreating back. "I was only asking."

By the time she reached the trailer, Amber was shaking with disappointment and rage.

"Never mind pet," her mother consoled her, "I think you were just a bit too ambitious in the jump-off. You're not experienced enough yet to be making tight turns into jumps that size. You can start having your lessons again and you and Molly will be winning all sorts soon."

"Yeah," Emily joined in, holding Molly while Amber removed the saddle, "you did really well. It can take ages to bond with a new pony. Don't worry about it."

But Amber *did* worry. If Molly was supposed to be such a wonderful jumper, surely she should've been able to manage that double? Amber was plagued by the thought that it had been her fault and Molly would have jumped with a better rider. Elisha's words still stung her. The girl had a knack of pinpointing what she was thinking and feeling like a mind reader. Her mood blackened even further when it was announced that Elisha had come first and second in both of the biggest classes on North Quest and Thunder Cat.

"I will beat her one day," Amber vowed to herself, "if it's the last thing I do."

- Jen -

Trojan Horse

"She's certainly a looker." Claire ran her hands over Molly's smooth, hard shoulders that shone like polished wood, before running experienced fingers down Molly's legs. "Plenty of heart room, deep chest, clean legs. Yep, she's a beauty." She stood back to admire the overall picture in front of her. "But you say she's bolted with you and didn't jump too well on Sunday?"

They were standing in the outdoor arena at Pine Tree Stables, ready to start Amber's first lesson with Molly. Gloomily, Amber recounted the terrifying ride through the forest and the abysmal jump-off round at the weekend. Claire listened intently, never taking her eyes off Molly as Amber talked. It was as if she was trying to communicate telepathically with the pony; to see into her mind and read her thoughts.

"And then Elisha Templeton was nasty to me again. I'm sure she saw me jumping but pretended not to just so she could ask how I'd done, to see what I would say. So, I've got to get better so I can beat her," Amber finished, resolutely.

Claire didn't reply immediately. She remained fixed to the spot, scrutinising Molly with a slight frown on her face. "What was her last rider like?"

"Erm, in what way?" Asked Amber, surprised by the question.

"Well, you know: tall, small, light, heavy, timid, bold?"

Amber thought of Frankie. She pictured her astride the mighty Bonfire Bob and remembered what she'd heard people say about her.

"Well, I suppose you'd say Frankie was quite stocky and strong – taller than me. She's pretty confident as she rode her mum's horse when I tried Molly and he was a massive handful. And I suppose she must be quite competitive because she's won loads of rosettes and trophies."

Claire nodded, taking in the information shrewdly. "Did you ever see her ride Molly? Did she show her off before you tried her?"

"No, it was just me. She was brought out of the stable, we rode round the block then I jumped a tiny jump in a really tiny arena – it was a chicken yard really – and that was it."

"Did you ask if you could have her on trial before making a decision?"

"We did ask but they said someone else was interested in her and would definitely have her if we didn't want her, so they said no."

"Hmmm." Claire continued to stand with one hand on her hip, gazing blankly at nothing in particular as if she had forgotten where she was and what she was doing. "Right then," she said briskly, breaking out of her trance. "Let's see her in action."

Amber took Molly through her paces while Claire sat on the fence, watching but offering no comment. This was unusual for her, Amber thought, as she was usually a very attentive instructor who offered a constant stream of advice to help the pupil improve their riding. Still without speaking,

Claire climbed down from the fence and erected four small jumps, including a double.

"Shorten your stirrups and try these," she instructed.

Amber pulled her stirrups up two holes and they cantered easily over the small jumps. Silently, Claire put the jumps up so that they were about eighty centimetres and told Amber to come again. Once more Molly cantered smoothly to the jumps and went over them with little effort. Amber patted her gratefully. She was jumping so well, Amber started to think she must've dreamt Sunday's disaster.

"Well done, you're riding really nicely," commented Claire as she jiggled a stiff cup on the fence nearest her. "Now, let's have them up a bit more and see how you manage."

Amber walked Molly around the arena for a few laps as she watched Claire adjust the jumps. She had put them up to about ninety centimetres and fences two and three had been pushed together to make a spread.

"Okay," Claire called to signal the jumps were ready. Just as before, Molly cantered gracefully around the arena, but she went over the first jump rather awkwardly and

Amber landed back in the saddle with a bang. Wincing slightly from the jarring landing, Amber rode on towards the spread fence. Molly felt different this time. Instead of moving on and jumping easily, she was backing off and trying to veer off the line Amber was riding. Amber tried to use her legs to keep Molly straight, but she was not strong enough and Molly ran out at the last minute. Claire, who had been watching from the fence, jumped down and waved at Amber to wait.

"You're going to have to be very firm with her," the instructor advised, "her last rider was strong and confident. You are a very gentle rider, which is good, but you do need a bit more drive to persuade her to do these bigger jumps. Start again and really ride her positively."

Amber nodded and gathered her reins up, noticing that they were suddenly slicked with sweat. Looking down at Molly's neck beneath her she could see the pony's coat was dark and wet. *That's funny,* she thought, *she wasn't sweaty at all a minute ago.* Giving it no further thought, she rode Molly strongly onward and slapped her shoulder with the stick as they approached the first fence. Molly jumped but Amber heard the pole fall as they landed. At the spread, Molly attempted to jump but caught the pole heavily with her hind legs and brought it crashing down, and she refused at the double. Amber re-presented her three times, but Molly wouldn't jump and eventually refused to even go near the fence, backing up and shaking her head. Amber's face was burning with frustration and the effort of trying to stop Molly from going backwards. She was getting redder and redder as she tried harder to get Molly moving in the right direction when Claire called to her. "Stop Amber, stop!"

Drained of all energy, Amber gratefully slumped back in the saddle, her head beating and hot inside her hard hat. "What am I–"

"Has this pony ever had an injury to its back?" Claire interrupted.

"She jumped through a wall after standing on her bandages a couple of years ago and hurt her back, but we had her vetted and he said her back was okay." Amber puffed.

"I'd get a second opinion if I were you," said Claire, exhaling deeply. "She wasn't happy at all when the jumps went up. She looked uncomfortable once the poles went higher. She might just have some niggling problem that doesn't bother her when the jumps are small, but she can really feel it when she has to stretch more for bigger ones."

Claire saw the dejection in Amber's face and body and knew how she was feeling. No sooner had she got herself a good competition pony after slogging away with reluctant little Pearl than it looked like Molly would be out of action for a while. The instructor patted Amber on the leg. "Don't worry. I've got a number for a very good chiropractor. With a bit of treatment and some rest, I'm sure you'll be jumping brilliantly in no time."

Amber didn't look convinced.

"Think of it like this. A pony trying to jump with a bad back is like you doing PE in trainers a size too small. You could put up with it for a while but eventually, you'd be in agony. If you knew it would be the same every PE lesson, you'd soon start avoiding the class completely. From Molly's point of view, if she feels pain every time she jumps, she'll soon stop jumping altogether, even small ones, because she'll associate pain with jumping. But get her treated now and she'll probably be happy to jump again. Come and get this number."

***

Eddie 'the back man' couldn't come for two weeks, so Molly was allowed to rest while they waited, and Amber went back to riding Pearl in the meantime. As Fudge was now approved for riding by the vet, Emily didn't come back to ride Honey again. The only upside was that Amber could ride out with Joanne again now that she was so much better. Sometimes her mum or dad joined them, other times, one of them took Honey out on her own to get her out of 'riding school mode,' as she was still apt to tuck in behind another pony and hide from any horrors lurking on the way.

It seemed strange now to go back to riding Pearl. The difference between her and Molly was huge. Getting back on Pearl was like sitting back in an old comfortable chair, where she could relax with the familiarity of knowing its feel and where the stains were and that she could put her feet up and drop things without worrying about marking it. In comparison, Molly was like a new, tall, hard, straight-backed chair where she had to sit up straight, behave properly, and do everything right. Amber knew that Molly was a classy pony and she needed more time to get used to her, but the bolt and the jumping disaster had unnerved her, and although she didn't want to admit it to herself, Molly had frightened her. Amber was glad for an excuse to not ride her for a couple of weeks.

It was nice to talk to Joanne again after not seeing her for so long, but she was surprised to find that Jo was not having such a good time at her school. She had been off for a couple of months after her accident and had fallen behind in some of her subjects. Amber didn't think it would matter much as Jo was still in Year Six; she was bright and would soon catch up. But the main problem wasn't really the work; it was the other kids.

"Some of them laugh at me and call me thick if I get stuck on work because I've missed what they've done earlier, so I don't know what to do."

"Doesn't your teacher know?" Amber asked, concerned for her friend.

"Not really, they do it when the teacher isn't looking, or they pass me notes. One girl, Megan, is really mean and passes notes either to me or about me saying horrible things."

Amber felt sympathetic towards Joanne as there were kids in her own form at her school who teased her and called her 'swot' or 'goofy' on account of her prominent front teeth. Especially Kieran and Josh, who seemed to think it necessary to say something unpleasant every time they saw her. It didn't bother her too much as they were such ugly boys – Kieran with his small, piggy eyes and Josh with his jug ears - that Amber wasn't much bothered what they thought of her. Especially as she knew her braces would eventually straighten her teeth. Sometimes, when they were taunting her and trying to humiliate her in front of others, she felt like saying something back to them to shut them up, but she never did. Something always held her back from retaliating, but she didn't know what. She wondered if Joanne stuck up for herself or just let it wash over her.

"Are you going to do anything about it?" she asked.

"Nah, she's stupid. She sends me notes saying how thick I am and nearly every word is spelt wrong. It's like a joke! I think she's just pleased that there's someone in the class doing worse than her, but it won't last long. I'll get my revenge when I start catching up and *she's* still at the bottom."

"I like your style," Amber smiled to herself, impressed at Joanne's positive attitude, "do you want to canter here?"

***

Two weeks sailed by in no time, and soon Eddie was pulling up in his pick-up to examine Molly's back. When Amber saw him lumbering down the yard, built like a rhinoceros, it was clear he had done a lot of hard work in his life. His shoulders were square and solid, his arms heavily muscled and his hands calloused and leathery. He had untidy, greying hair and a crooked nose that looked like it had been broken more than once. But despite his rather untoward appearance, he smiled warmly at the Andersons and softly exchanged the necessary pleasantries before turning his attention to Molly, who was tied up and eating from a haynet outside Honey and Pearl's shared stable. Eddie rolled up his sleeves, revealing his mighty forearms, and after asking what problems they'd been having with Molly, he placed his hands on her back and began his examination. His fingers probed along her spine, along her neck and between her ears, where he lingered a while, rubbing and prodding. Molly, completely unperturbed, carried on sleepily munching her hay. Then Eddie moved to stand directly behind Molly and placed his fingertips on her hip bones. He pressed gently around her pelvis, peered down her spine and lifted her tail to assess the movement of her dock. All this was carried out in silence, with Amber and her parents watching in mute fascination. The only noise was the rhythmical grinding of Molly's teeth on the hay she was eating.

Eventually, the silence was broken as Eddie gave Molly a hearty slap on the rump and turned to face his customers.

"Well, there's nowt wrong wid tha pony's back. She's a la'l bit tight in her poll, but I don't think that would be causing the problems you've described." He wiped his hands on a cloth to remove the grease from them. The Andersons weren't sure whether this was good news or not. They were obviously pleased Molly wasn't in pain, but then if pain wasn't causing her problems, what was the cause?

Eddie ran both hands over his head in a vain attempt to smooth his hair but as soon as he let go, it fell into his eyes again. Amber thought he looked like an Old English Sheepdog.

"But it was her back that was injured a couple of years ago," protested Mrs Anderson, "it must be that. She hasn't had any other injuries."

"You said she stood on an unravelled bandage when she hurt herself, is that right?"

"Yes."

"Well, I'm no vet, but it could be that when she stood on the bandage, it became very tight around the front leg. If it wasn't removed immediately it could've caused some damage to the tissues surrounding the flexor tendon in that leg. A too tight bandage can cut off the blood supply."

Mr Anderson frowned and rubbed his chin, "But if it had been a tendon back then, wouldn't her leg have swelled up and she'd have been lame? They'd have noticed. Like now, if it was a tendon, she'd be lame wouldn't she, and she isn't."

Eddie shrugged, "Like I said, mate, I'm not a vet, but I've been around horses long enough to know their injuries aren't always obvious or straightforward. If there is an old injury, it probably isn't bad enough to make her lame now, but it could be that she didn't get enough time for it fully heal. It could have been very slight and not even showed up, but it might still niggle at her and she'll probably feel it more when she has to jump bigger fences and the landing is more jarring. That could explain her lack of enthusiasm for jumping when they get bigger, but like I said, I'm not a vet. As for the bolting, well, sorry lass," he looked at Amber and smiled apologetically, "that likely has nowt to do with pain and plenty to do with excitement and a light, inexperienced rider she can run off with." He smiled again. "Maybe you should use a stronger bit if you're going out in a group. In the meantime, she needs a few days of just light work to allow those poll muscles to settle down again."

Eddie was thanked for his time and drove away, loudly chased by Kelly and Tess the farm dogs.

"Well, that wasn't what we expected to hear." Mrs Anderson sighed with frustration. "Camp is less than two weeks away and now the pony we've bought for these things might not be fit to go."

Amber led Molly back into the stable – her shoulders slumped – and pulled the door shut behind her. She could still hear her parents' frustrated voices as she gently teased a knot from Molly's silky mane. Amber thought about all the dreams she'd had about winning competitions, beating people like Elisha and riding round in glorious splendour. Those hopes now looked as far away as ever. Molly had seemed like such a prize when she'd arrived, but now Amber wasn't so sure.

***

The evening meal that night was much more subdued than usual, with each person lost in their own private thoughts while Kasper watched each mouthful hopefully, waiting for a tasty scrap and wondering why everyone was so quiet. Eventually, Mr Anderson cleared his throat and spoke. "Did you call the vet?" he asked his wife.

"Yes, someone's coming on Thursday."

"Right."

"God knows what it'll cost."

"Mmm."

Silence ruled over the remainder of the meal, and Kasper slunk off to bed, miserably aware that his legendary begging was not going be rewarded tonight.

-Eleven-

Emily Strikes Back

The bespectacled Irish vet carried out a variety of upper and lower leg flexion tests, which revealed little more than a tiny amount of stiffness in Molly's front left leg after a prolonged period of flexion. He dismissed it as being nothing.

"Seems unlikely she has any tendon problems," he lilted softly, "but we can't x-ray it as that would only show us her bones. If she was lame, we could try nerve blocks, but she's moving fine."

"So, what can we do?" Mrs Anderson asked.

The vet took off his glasses and wiped them on his sleeve. "There's no heat, swelling or lameness, so there isn't really any treatment I can suggest other than to rest her. I'd recommend you don't ride her for a month and after that, light hacking and even showing if she's well-schooled enough, but no jumping for six months. A good rest might be all she needs."

After the vet left, with Kelly and Tess once again noisily escorting his vehicle off the farmyard, Mrs Anderson curled her fists in a Hulk-like frustration.

Amber recognised the rising colour in her mother's face as a sign she was getting stressed and tried to calm her down before she blew up. "It's hard for them to know what's wrong when animals can't tell them what the problem is."

Mrs Anderson was turning puce. "Yes, I know but he was as useful as a…" she clearly couldn't think of anything useless enough to compare the vet to, and left the sentence hanging.

Amber didn't know whether to say that she had a horrible suspicion that the recent gallop over rocky ground on the ride when Molly bolted, followed by the tight turns she'd ridden in the jump-offs at the recent show might have caused an injury to her new pony. She opened her mouth to suggest it, but guilt seemed to block the words, and nothing came out.

Mrs Anderson's slate blue eyes sharpened in her flushed face, her muscles taut and her mouth set in a thin, hard line. Despite knowing her daughter was right, it didn't help her temper to pass. Molly had been recommended to them and they'd had high hopes for her. After watching Amber struggle with Pearl last year, trying to compete against ponies like Rocky and Flash, she and her husband had been looking forward to watching Amber have an easier and more successful season this year. But now they had three ponies to keep and pay for, and not one of them was suitable for competitions. They definitely couldn't manage with four, so it looked like her daughter's hopes were doomed. She sighed heavily, the anger suddenly leaving her like an unwanted evil spirit, leaving her body feeling tired and unfamiliar. "I don't know what you're going to do about camp. Molly can't go so it looks like you'll have to take Pearl."

Amber nodded, accepting the inevitable, until the recent memory of Emily jumping Honey and the pony's joyful performance gave Amber a sudden idea. "I could take Honey to camp!"

"What? Honey?" Mrs Anderson was surprised. "Oh no, I don't think Honey would be very good. You know she's nervous and she's hardly done any jumping. You'd be better off on Pearl."

"She's a lot braver these days, Mum, and anyway, she's only nervous on rides. She was great jumping with Emily. You know I love Pearl, but you can see Honey likes to jump – she enjoys it! Pearl would hate a week of jumping every day. Too much effort! Please, Mum, let me take Honey. She'll be fine."

And so, it was decided. Honey was going to camp.

***

Amber was so excited about her first Pony Club camp, she could barely contain herself as they unloaded Honey from the trailer, her eyes popping as she wondered where on earth she was. Highland Park Equestrian Centre, near Carlisle, was a large, professional establishment. Amber had never been before, but as she stood looking around, she took in the cross-country fences in distant fields, brightly painted show jumps, the two indoor arenas, and the beautiful stable blocks.

The stables were in clusters around the yard. Three to ten boxes were built inside small barns, each containing their own supplies of hay, shavings and mucking out equipment. The centre's own horses had been temporarily moved to the livery quarters or turned out to graze to make room for the Pony Club. Each stable door had the name of a member's pony blu-tacked over the usual occupant's name. Amber found Honey's in a small block of three stables. The stall next to hers belonged to Fudge, and next to that was Breeze, Kate's small bay horse. As she led a very surprised Honey into her stable, Emily's head popped up from the one next door.

The walls between them were thick wooden panels to shoulder height, and on top of them, metal railings extended another three feet so that the occupants of the stables could see into the one beside them.

"Hello neighbour," she greeted Amber with a smile. "It's great our stables are next to each other isn't it? Now Honey and Fudgey can make friends."

"Amber laughed, "How is he now?"

"Oh, fully healed and raring to go, thanks." She planted a big kiss on Fudge's soft muzzle and ruffled his thick blond forelock affectionately, grinning happily at Amber. Amber chuckled again and removed Honey's head collar, allowing the pony to sniff and paw inquisitively at the bed of shavings, which she'd probably never seen before.

"I thought you'd be bringing Molly to camp?" Emily said in a questioning tone.

"Oh, I know," Amber replied with a shrug, "it's a long story…"

There was little time to notice everyone else as members rushed around, unpacking their riding gear, tack, feed buckets, grooming kits and everything else they'd brought for the week. Soon it was time to tack up for the first ride.

"Make sure everything's spotless," Emily advised, "we're judged on turnout every day and the best person out of all the groups gets a trophy at the end."

"Thanks for telling me." Amber hurriedly shoved her long blonde hair into a hairnet and checked her tie was straight in the hazy reflection of the barn window.

"Ah, excellent, you're all here." Mrs Best appeared loudly in the doorway. "Just here to tell you all which ride you're in. Now, we have three groups, based on you and your pony's experience and level of competition." She looked into Breeze's stable, where the small, dark-skinned Kate was tightening the girth. "Kate, I know you were in the top group on the ponies but as your new horse is only a baby, we've put you in the second group. I hope you don't mind that?"

"No, that's fine," the girl replied, "it's what I expected."

"Jolly good. Now, Emily, you'll also be in group two and Amber..." The large, bubbly DC turned to face Amber, "we weren't quite sure where to put you dear as neither you nor your pony have a lot of experience but I think we'll try you in group two as well, although you might need to drop into group three, but we'll wait and see how you get on." She clapped her hands together. "See you all mounted up and ready to go in five minutes."

Soon, the riders of groups two and three were all assembled in the large indoor arena having their tack and turnout inspection. The top group were out of sight in the adjoining smaller arena.

"I thought I saw Natalie earlier," Emily leaned over and whispered to Amber, "but she's not here."

Amber looked up and down the line of riders in her group and also at the other riders who were now occupying the bottom half of the arena.

"No, you're right," she whispered back, "perhaps there's some problem with Sable, so she can't ride?"

Emily shrugged and pulled a quizzical face, ceasing the conversation as the instructor approached for her tack inspection.

***

When the lesson was complete and everyone's tack was cleaned and put away and the ponies were fed and brushed, it was time for the riders to get ready for tea. Amber, Emily, Kate and three other girls were sleeping in an old tack room where odds and ends were stored. They all had camp beds and sleeping bags, and their possessions were already mixed up and strewn around the tiny room.

"Has anyone seen my mug? It's blue." Emily asked.

"And where's my other trainer?" cried Becky, a red-haired girl of about fourteen.

Eventually, everybody found their lost items and crammed all their stuff under their beds before making their way to the large classroom which sat between the two indoor arenas for their meal.

Amber and Emily collected their pizza and oven chips from the mums who were staying to help, and then looked for somewhere to sit.

"Hey, there's Natalie sitting over there with Elisha. Come on." Emily nudged Amber and walked over to join them. Amber grudgingly followed, not relishing the thought of eating with Elisha.

"Hi!" Emily greeted them, plonking herself down opposite them. "So where were you earlier? How come you weren't riding?" she asked Natalie. But before Natalie could get a word out, Elisha answered for her. "She *was* riding."

"Oh, it's just that we didn't see you." Emily frowned.

"No, well she's in the top group, that's why."

Amber and Emily exchanged a disbelieving look. "Oh, right. Well done, Natalie," Emily offered politely.

"Thanks. I'm not on Sable obviously though. If I'd brought her, I'd be in the bottom group."

"No?"

"No, we've decided to sell her... if we can get anyone to buy her, and get a new one. And Elisha is selling her pony, Rocky, so we've arranged for me to try him here all this week and if I like him, we'll buy him."

"You're joking?" Amber blurted out.

"No, why?" Natalie looked crestfallen that her news hadn't received a more exciting response.

"Yeah, Amber," Elisha fixed Amber with her penetrating stare, "have you got a problem with that?"

"No, um, er, nothing, sorry," Amber muttered and looked down.

"So, Nat, is today the first time you've ridden him then?" Emily continued, helpfully removing everyone's attention from Amber.

"I've only ridden him once before at Elisha's – we went for a hack – and today we did flatwork, so I haven't jumped him yet, but I can already tell how much different he is to Sable. He's so forward going. It's great. I'm having to hold him back instead of kicking and pushing all the time. I can't wait till we start jumping tomorrow."

Amber felt her eyebrow raise involuntarily at Natalie's naïve enthusiasm. Sure, it was great to have a livelier pony after the deathly lethargic Sable, but had she forgotten that Rocky had bolted with Elisha and subsequently broke her ankle when he fell on her last year? Or did she even know about it? Amber wondered if Elisha and her father had deliberately failed to mention Rocky's strength and unpredictably, in order to take advantage of the Riley's inexperience, to make a sale. She had no doubt that they were both devious enough. After her own recent, terrifying experience with Molly, she knew she needed to warn Natalie that Rocky was dangerous. She needed to find a way to get Natalie away from Elisha so that she could speak to her privately. But how? Her mind raced as Emily kept talking.

"That's a big step for you then, Nat, 'cause if you're in the top group you compete in the Open at the end of week One Day Event. A one-metre cross-country course will be a challenge on a pony you're not used to," Emily said, her voice heavy with concern.

"Oh, shut up, you're only jealous 'cause you're both stuck in group two on your fat little hair-balls," Elisha spat nastily. "You've been competing for years and still haven't got past ninety centimetres. That's why you're jealous," she said, jabbing a finger at Emily, "because Natalie is getting a brilliant new pony and you're still on Fat Fudge even though you're too big for him. What's up? Can't Mummy and Daddy afford a new one?"

Emily's kind, rosy face drained of colour and hardened like stone. Her soft, gentle eyes narrowed and glinted menacingly as she slowly leaned forward and put her face right up to Elisha's.

"You think you're so wonderful, don't you, looking down your nose at everyone because your dad has loads of money from his dodgy dealings and your ponies are always the best bred and most expensive in the country? *That's* the only reason you've done well in competitions, Elisha, because you're a crap rider. You've had push button ponies that have done it all for you since you started. You couldn't get a thing out of a pony like Fudge or Honey because you only know how to sit there and get carried around. And as for Natalie riding Rocky, no offence Natalie – you and your dad know he's too much for her – she's only eleven and not very experienced, but you don't care so long as you get your money."

Amber and Natalie stared in shocked silence as the normally friendly, easy-going Emily retaliated with force against Elisha. Even Elisha was momentarily taken aback to find Emily's face inches from her own throughout the verbal onslaught. She soon regained her composure and flung back at Emily loudly, "Don't make me laugh! *I* couldn't ride your pathetic second rate ponies? I wouldn't lower myself to their sub-zero standard. I think you'll find it's *you* who couldn't ride *my* ponies, who are *not* push button, they are highly strung, sensitive and so well-schooled they need very precise, skilled riding. And as for our parents, at least *my* dad has money. What does your dad do again? Oh no, I forgot, he doesn't have a job, does he?"

Quick as a flash, Emily lunged forward and dealt Elisha a stinging slap across the face. The loud thwack resounded around the echoey room and all heads turned to stare incredulously just as Elisha grabbed a handful of Emily's curly dark hair and proceeded to twist it until Emily squealed. Amber and Natalie both tried frantically to release Elisha's grip on Emily's hair, but it took the two mothers, who had been filling beakers with orange squash, to leap into action and separate the sparring girls.

As soon as she was free from Elisha's vice-like grip, Emily sprang away from the table, toppling her chair as she pushed it roughly out of her way, and ran headlong out of the building, across the dusty yard and into the small barn where Honey, Fudge and Breeze were stabled. Amber followed immediately before any interrogations began, and found her friend sobbing pitifully on a bale of hay. Her sudden noisy intrusion had startled the ponies and they were all looking at her, wide-eyed over their stable doors.

"Are you okay?" Amber gasped breathlessly, sitting down close to Emily, feeling her icy skin covered in goose bumps as sobs shuddered through her body. "I can't believe you stood up to Elisha! You were so brave. I wish I could be like that. I never know what to say in an argument, I always say something useless and end up looking totally stupid. What you said was absolutely true."

"And look where it got me," Emily snapped. "I hardly won the battle, did I?"

"But…" Amber couldn't think what to say. How could she let Emily know how much she admired her for standing up for herself against a bully like Elisha while she sat there and said nothing? "But you didn't lose anything. You showed her you're not scared of her and she can't just say what she likes to you."

"But she did say what she liked, didn't she? She said I'm too big for Fudge, I still jump at Intermediate level and my dad doesn't have a job at the moment. Everything she said was true too."

Amber put an arm around Emily's shaking shoulders. "Firstly, you're not too big for Fudge – he's stocky and you're not heavy – so he won't even feel you, and so what if you don't jump Opens? You're only thirteen and Fudge is only just over thirteen hands; you've got loads of time to progress. Everyone in the top group, apart from Elisha and Natalie, is at least fourteen and like you said, Elisha only does Opens because she has great ponies, not because she's a good rider. And so what if your dad has lost his job? He'll get another one."

Emily sniffed and rubbed her eyes, "He's been trying, but nobody seems to be taking anyone new on."

The girls continued talking and gradually Emily calmed down and stopped crying. Presently, Mrs Best found them, still sitting in the barn in semi-darkness, and asked what had happened. To her credit, she listened without interrupting and when she went away, she was shaking her head and muttering to herself.

Emily didn't feel like joining in the evening quiz and having everyone stare at her, so they went to bed early and fell into an exhausted sleep well before the other girls returned and crept into their cramped camp beds.

Trust Elisha to go and spoil things before we've hardly begun, was Amber's last thought before she fell into a deep and dreamless sleep.

-Twelve-

A Whale of a Time

The next morning saw all the riders assembled in their groups for show jumping instruction. Kate, seated on Breeze, yawned and looked at Amber. "Did you know your pony kept everyone awake last night? she asked, stretching.

"What, Honey? No, why, what did she do?"

"Are you kidding? She banged on the stable door all night long. Don't tell me you didn't hear it?"

"No, honestly I didn't. I'm really sorry but she's not used to being kept in a stable and she could be missing our other pony as well."

"Well, you must sleep like the dead. I got up and Chelsea came with me to see what was making the racket.

134

We gave her more hay in case she was banging 'cause she was hungry, but as soon as we came back to bed, she started again. I just hope she's not going to do it every night."

After the tack inspection, group three went to use the outdoor arena, leaving Amber's group with the whole of the large indoor school to themselves.

"Now, as you all know, you will be competing against each other in the One Day Event at the end of the week. This afternoon I will be giving you all a copy of the dressage test you will perform. We will have some time to practise it every day, but in accordance with British Eventing rules, you must memorise the test and perform it accurately with no outside assistance. Any errors in the sequence of the test will incur penalties," Jilly, the instructor, a tweed-jacketed, plain-faced lady, told the group formally. "But as we did flatwork yesterday, our lesson this morning will be show jumping. The show jumps and cross-country fences on Friday will be eighty-five centimetres, so that is the height we will be practising at. Now, I need to get some wings and poles out, so I'd like you all to go and work in, do plenty of transitions and get your ponies relaxed and listening to you.

And remember to pass each other left shoulder to left shoulder. Look where you're going, we don't want any crashes."

The six riders began warming up, easily managing to avoid each other in the huge space. Suddenly, as Amber trotted Honey across the centre of the arena, the pony caught sight of herself in the mirror on the wall and uttered a welcoming 'huh huh huh' at her reflection. Amber chuckled. "No girl, that's yourself, it's not Pearl." She caught Emily grinning at her and smiled back. Then, as they trotted around the corner and down the long side, there was another mirror, strategically placed to allow riders to see how straight they were sitting and the position of the horse as it travelled down the line. Honey spied her reflection again and whinnied deeply once more. This time the whole group laughed, and Amber patted the black neck affectionately. "You silly girl."

After that, Honey whinnied at her reflection every time she passed a mirror until the other riders were groaning at her to be quiet. Eventually Amber had to ride so that she was always moving away from the mirrors instead of riding towards them to keep the confused pony quiet.

Fortunately, when the jumping began, Honey was too busy enjoying herself and concentrating on the fences to notice the mirrors. Jilly had put up a short course of a steep-sided cross pole, a gate, a parallel and a double. Each rider had to jump the course shouting out each stride they took in between the fences. Amber found this exercise very useful as she'd never fully understood strides, but counting out loud, 'one – two – three – four -,' in between the jumps helped her to judge her take-off position much better.

"Well done Amber," the instructor patted Honey's already damp neck, "you've got a very game pony there. She's really making an effort for you. Now, at the moment you're getting five strides between fence three and the double, but she's arriving at the double rather flat and's having to make a big effort to clear it. This time, hold her to six strides but still use your legs for impulsion, then she should arrive at the double more in balance and with more bounce so the jumps will be easier for her."

Amber always listened carefully and soon found that the instructor was spot on with her advice. Every time she did what Jilly told her, her performance improved. By the end of the session, both pony and rider were glowing with happiness.

Honey was so willing and easy to ride, and Amber could tell how much she was enjoying this new activity that had crept unexpectedly into her life. It made such a difference to her own enjoyment when riding a pony that was so obviously enthusiastic.

The afternoon's lesson of dressage test practice was harder than Amber thought it would be. Honey's walk and trot were very good, but she ran into canter and was quite unbalanced, especially in the corners. By the end of the session, Amber was dripping with sweat as Jilly had been determined to improve Honey's canter strike off, and had made Amber go over and over it until she was satisfied. In fact, she had spent so much time concentrating on Honey's canter that she hadn't yet practised any of the dressage test. Amber was sure she wouldn't be able to remember all of the test on Friday. She still couldn't remember all of her seven or eight times tables, and they were just a list of numbers that could be recited in thirty seconds. If she couldn't manage that, how on earth was she going to memorise a four-minute test where she had to remember paces, transitions, circles, changes of rein, letters, halts and salutes? And the descriptions of the movements were so wordy, by the time she'd read the first few movements, she'd forgotten the first one.

"Emily, what does 'change the rein on a long rein H x F' mean?" She waggled the test sheet under her friend's nose later that afternoon and Emily laughed at her panicked expression.

"Come here, I'll show you how to learn a dressage test." Emily drew a rectangle on a piece of paper to represent the arena and quickly labelled the lettered markers around it.

"So, the order of letters is A, K, E, H, C, M, B and F." She pointed them out with her pencil. "The way to remember them is 'All King Edward's Horses Can Move Bloomin' Fast', " she shared. "Right, enter at A in working trot. Proceed down the centre line without halting and track left."

As Emily read each movement, she explained to Amber what it meant and drew a faint dotted line to represent it on the paper. When they came to a part in the test where you had to canter a 20-metre circle, Emily switched to an unbroken line, taking care not to draw over the dotted line. For the few movements in walk, she drew a wiggly line.

"There. That helps you to remember what you're doing where. Now go through it a few times and only look at the instructions if you really need to."

Amber followed Emily's sketch and was surprised to find she remembered quite a lot of it.

"Good, now come on." Emily grabbed Amber's hand and pulled her up off her camp bed.

"Where're we going?"

"To practise!" Emily's eyes twinkled.

Soon Amber found herself in one of the outdoor arenas, minus a pony, trotting and cantering her way through the test on foot.

"This is stupid," she giggled as she cantered past Emily, who was sitting on the gate with the test in her hand. "I hope nobody sees me doing this."

"Don't worry about that. You were supposed to trot *at* F, not after F. You'll lose marks if you're not accurate."

"Oh damn." Amber stopped to catch her breath. "Hang on, I'll do it again in a minute."

That night was the most restless night's sleep Amber had ever had. Unable to switch off from committing the test to memory, she ran through it in her head all night long, seeing herself trotting around the arena in her mind. She probably called out 'between C and M working canter right…' and her legs must have been joining in with her thoughts as her sleeping bag was twisted around her like a boa constrictor when she awoke in the morning. She felt so weary during breakfast that she was sure she would fall asleep during her first cross-country lesson.

***

Wednesday and Thursday flew by with more training in the three disciplines required for the One Day Event. Amber absolutely loved cross-country. They practised over most of the fences that would be part of the course on Friday.

"We'll leave a few out to make the competition a bit more interesting," Jilly said.

They started by tackling one fence at a time, then they linked a few together before Jilly improvised a longer course for them to ride.

"This won't be the course on Friday, so make sure you walk it properly on the day, so you know where you're going."

Jilly set them off one at a time, waiting until the rider on the course had finished before setting the next one off. Amber loved the feeling of being alone, with no-one watching as she rode Honey around the course, feeling the rhythm of her stride and the sound of her hooves striking the earth.

Some of the ponies in the group had refused to jump the ditch in the coffin fence and quite a few didn't want to go through the water jump. Even Fudge had wavered and baulked on his approach, as the water was quite muddy, and the bottom couldn't be seen. Jilly had called on Amber and Honey to give some of the reluctant ponies a lead, to encourage them to follow Honey over the jumps. Amber couldn't keep the smile off her face at being used as the lead rider in the group, and her confidence soared.

Now, as Amber rode the course, over the ditch, up the steps, over the double of logs and through the water, she felt so pleased she'd brought Honey to camp. She thought about what her parents would think when she told them how scaredy cat Honey had been used as a lead to get other ponies to jump.

Honey tired towards the end of the course but gamely jumped the last few fences and returned to a round of applause from the group.

"Clear round! Well done Amber and well done Honey!"

Amber was walking on air for the remaining days as Honey continued to jump well, and she found that she could remember the dressage test every time they practised it. Her mood was further lifted when Emily gleefully pulled her into a corner and whispered that cross-country training hadn't gone so well for Elisha. Thunder Cat had refused to jump the ditch and wouldn't even walk into the water jump, never mind jump into it as the Open class had to. Nor would he jump off the Irish bank. Elisha had sat on top of the bank, kicking and whipping until eventually, the young black horse had reared up. In the end, Elisha had to dismount and help the instructor attach a lunge rein to him. They then managed to coax him down from the ground.

Things had gone just as badly for Natalie, as Rocky had run away with her all over the fields, and when he did go over the fences, he'd jumped so fast and with so much power, he'd thrown Natalie right out of the saddle. When Amber heard this, she felt awful. She'd had every intention of warning Natalie about Rocky but hadn't been able to speak to her without Elisha being around. Unlike Emily, Amber always withered in Elisha's presence, and so Natalie remained unaware of what was in store for her.

The result of this was that both girls had been told they would compete in the Intermediate class on Friday instead of in the Open. Natalie was very happy with this decision but Elisha was apparently fuming and had started her 'do you know how much this horse cost?' speech, only to be told by their instructor that she didn't care how much he had cost, or how he was bred – he was only a five-year-old and didn't need to be frightened while he was still a baby.

"You can't just expect to take an untrained young horse round a metre cross-country course, even if he is show jumping that height. Cross-country training needs to be taken slowly to build his confidence. If you lose his trust now, he'll *never* make an eventer. He's not a ready-made pony like you're used to, Elisha. You're going to have to put a lot of time in to get him to the standard you're hoping to achieve."

"Wow... did her instructor *really* say that to her?" Amber asked Emily.

"That's what Alice, who's in her group, told me. And now she's spat her dummy out and is having a major sulk. She said some nasty things to Natalie too about not being able to ride Rocky properly."

"What a surprise."

"So, you know what that means now?"

Amber's eyebrows knitted together, and she shook her head.

"It means we'll be competing against her. We've got a chance to beat her and her posh horse with our native no-hopers, as she calls them. Oh, wouldn't that be brilliant?" Emily squeezed her eyes tight shut and did a little excited jig.

145

Amber shook her head. "What do you mean? As if we could beat her. If she's been moved down a group, the dressage and show jumping will be even easier for her. She'll get a huge head start."

"Ah ha, yes, but if she gets eliminated on the cross-country, which she probably will, as our course has ditches and water that her horse doesn't like, her score won't count. She'll be finished. And even if she just gets a few stops on the course, it's twenty penalties for a refusal cross-country. Whatever you get in the dressage, all you have to do is get round the show jumping and cross-country and you'll beat her."

"Really?"

"Yup, really!"

-Thirteen-

A Rider's Responsibility

On Friday morning, Amber was one of the first out of bed. She mucked out the stable quickly then led Honey out and washed her legs and tail before the battle for the hosepipe began. At breakfast she pored over the dressage test again, willing her brain not to forget it. Her stomach began to squirm with anticipation as she thought that this could be the day her dream of beating Elisha came true. She laughed to herself at the thought of potentially achieving what seemed like the impossible on nervous little Honey. If it was ever going to happen, she'd thought it would be on Molly. The very idea of Honey triumphing over the super talented Thunder Cat gave her a slightly hysterical, lightheaded feeling.

Pushing her uneaten breakfast away and pulling herself together, she went back to the barn and cleaned her tack again. Then she rubbed and polished her riding boots until the soft leather gleamed. Next, she brushed her riding jacket and laid it out on her bed with a clean shirt and pair of jodhpurs, her hat, gloves and Pony Club tie. With all the tack and clothing prepared, she went back to the stable with the intention of making Honey look like the best pony there.

An hour later, Honey was immaculate. Her dark coat was lustrous, her heavy wavy tail was soft and sparkled with the baby oil Amber had brushed through it, and her mane was beautifully shown off in a crest plait Amber had recently learned how to do. All that was left was to oil her hooves, but Amber had discovered it was best not to do so in the stable as shavings and dust stuck to the oil.

She looked at her watch. The Open competitors would be doing their tests now. It had been arranged this way so that the Novice group, with the youngest members, would have longer to prepare and so that the older riders from the Open class could help them to get ready. Parents had been invited to watch the competition, and already some mums had arrived to organise their young offspring.

"Michael, where's your clean shirt?" Amber heard a harassed voice shriek. There was a pause followed by another strangled yell. "It's filthy and crumpled! Is it too much to ask for you to fold your clothes up and put them in your bag instead of leaving them on the floor? Look, it's even got a green footprint on this sleeve!"

With a smile and a small chuckle, Amber headed off to get changed herself.

**

Honey warmed up well, although her canter was still a bit rushed and unbalanced. Amber didn't worry about it though as she remembered Emily's advice. She could hear her now in her head saying, *Don't worry about the canter. The majority of the test is in trot, which is Honey's best pace. Just concentrate on being accurate, keep her straight on the long sides and don't let her fall in on the circles.*

Suddenly Emily was beside her on Fudge. He evidently didn't appreciate his bushy mane being forced into golf ball sized plaits and was shaking his head.

"I'm in next," she said.

"Good luck. I hope you do really well." Amber replied sincerely. She didn't know where she'd have been this week without all Emily's help and advice.

In no time Emily had finished her test and it was Amber's turn. The horn pipped and she entered the arena, trotting steadily up the centre line. She circled, changed rein, cantered and walked, all the time trying to execute the movements as accurately as she could. Soon she was trotting back up the centre line to halt and salute the judge. Honey gave her a lovely square halt, right on X. As she left the arena, she patted Honey and felt quite pleased with herself; she'd remembered it all and it seemed to have gone quite well. Her parents appeared and told her they'd seen her test.

"You did well – it was excellent for a first attempt," her dad said.

"I love Honey's mane." Mrs Anderson was stroking the pony's neck and examining the intricate looking plait. "She looks really elegant."

Amber was pleased they were there to watch her as she had a feeling it was going to be a good day.

The results from the dressage phase were pinned up just before the show jumping began. Amber and Emily checked their scores against the rest of the group. Elisha was in the lead with a very low penalty score of 23. A girl called Chelsea who rode a nice grey pony was second with 34. Jake was next with 36, Emily and Natalie both scored 44. Amber had 48. Kate was sixth with 50 and finally Ashley with 54.

Natalie was first to show jump in the Intermediate group and everyone watched with concern as she began her round. She did quite well really and finished with just four faults due to Rocky running straight past one of the fences. Next, Elisha jumped an effortless clear round, no doubt horrified at having to jump such insignificant fences. Kate got round on her young horse with one fence down, and then it was Emily's turn. She'd taken Fudge's plaits out after the dressage and now his thick mane was a mass of curls. He looked so cute with his blond curls bouncing as he jumped round, clearly enjoying himself, to equal Elisha's clear.

When Amber was called, she let out a long, trembling breath and entered the arena to begin her round. Honey felt keen and jumped the first fence enthusiastically. Fence after fence disappeared behind them as they continued to clear them all smoothly. Soon there was only the last left to jump. *We've gone clear,* thought Amber, relaxing as they approached the last fence. Feeling the slight change in her rider, Honey hesitated and put in an extra little shuffle before the fence and got too close to it. She tried to clear the jump, but she couldn't avoid clipping it and Amber heard the pole fall as they landed. *Thud.* Her own heart hit the ground at the same time as the pole as she realised she had cost them a clear round.

"Bad luck."

"What a shame."

Everyone was so disappointed when she re-joined them after her round and took her unhappy expression to be a sign of her own dismay at having a fence down. Amber's real disappointment though was not with Honey, or even about the fence, but the fact that she'd let her pony down, after she'd worked so hard all week, by not riding properly at the end. She'd thought the last fence would take care of itself and now she was kicking herself for denying Honey the clear round she deserved through bad riding.

She put Honey back in the stable and untacked her. After giving her a brush and taking out her plait, she held Honey's face in her hands. She smoothed her forelock, kissed her soft whiskery muzzle and looked firmly into the gentle brown eyes.

"I promise I won't let you down ever again," she told the pony.

"You giving that pony a pep talk?" Emily had suddenly appeared in the doorway and was amused to see Amber holding Honey's face, apparently giving her a good talking to.

"It's me that needs the pep talk," Amber mumbled, leaving the stable and flicking the kick bolt on with her foot, "not Honey."

"Come on then, let's go and walk the cross-country course."

The cross-country phase for all groups was to start after dinner, following the same pattern of Open riders going first. Emily led Amber to the start and showed her the map of the course.

"So, our class follows the blue numbers see, and that's our optimum time: four minutes and twenty seconds. That means you have to try to get round the course within that time. If you go over it, you get time penalties which are added to your score." Then Emily took her to the starting box which was marked out with white painted fencing and looked very professional. "This is where you'll start from. The starter will count you down and tell you to go. There's the first fence."

Amber looked and saw three brush jumps all in a horizontal line. They walked towards them.

"This one's ours." Emily patted the middle brush. "See the blue number? The Open has a red number one and the Novice's is green. And see these flags?" Emily indicated two flags on either side of the largest fence. "The course is set for the Open as they're first and these flags show them what they have to jump. You must always jump between the flags with the red one on your right. Red and right both start with R so it's easy to remember. For our class, they'll move the red flag out to the end of the middle jump so we can choose to jump either the middle or biggest one, okay?"

Amber nodded and they carried on. Emily was being an excellent course guide, her experience really showing as she explained how Amber should approach some of the fences, where she could save Honey's energy and where she'd need to push her more. They moved out of the field they'd practised in and came to a gate leading into a wooded area. It was flagged.

"You'll have to ride positively here as you're jumping from light into dark and a lot of ponies don't like it. Don't worry about that gate – it's set for the Open; we'll have a smaller one." Amber wondered how much smaller theirs would be as the current gate was enormous.

They continued through the wood where there were a few more scary new jumps and then into an open field that led back to the start. The finish was parallel to the start box. "Make sure you ride through the flags at the finish," Emily warned, "your time doesn't stop until you're through them so don't forget and miss them out."

By the time they got back to the yard and changed into their cross-country gear, Amber's stomach was clenching painfully, and she had forgotten part of the course. She'd been going over the fences in her head and couldn't remember the course from number eight to eleven. Emily tried to describe the fences, but she couldn't picture them properly.

"Don't worry, you'll be able to see the fences and their numbers as you're going round."

"Well, I can't actually," Amber admitted. "I can't see things in the distance very well. The fence numbers will be all blurred from horse height." She knew that she needed glasses as she struggled to see the board at school if she sat near the back, which she often did, but she hadn't got around to telling her parents yet.

Determined not to let Honey down twice in one day by forgetting the course, she knew she couldn't leave it to chance and hope for the best. It was her responsibility to make sure. "Will you put Honey's saddle on for me while I go back and have a quick look at the bit I've forgotten?" she asked Emily.

"Alright, but you haven't got very long. What about getting something to eat?" Emily was sitting on a bale of shavings eating a bacon sandwich. The smell turned Amber's stomach.

"Urgh, no thanks. I'll have something when I've finished. I'll run there and back, won't be long."

"Don't do that, you'll probably pass out or something. I'll tack Honey up for you and bring her out with Fudge. I'll meet you in the warm-up area."

"Oh thanks, you're great!"

Emily smiled. "I know."

With that, she set off to re-inspect the forgotten part of the course. On the way, she bumped into her parents who had been coming to the stable to see if she needed a hand. When she explained what she was doing, her mother offered to go and help Emily with the ponies. Her dad went with Amber to look at the jumps she'd forgotten. She told him all about the numbers and the flags – red to the right – and the time allowed and going through the finish.

"You certainly seem to have learned a lot this week," he said. "Have you enjoyed it?"

"Yeah, it's been great apart from Elisha. And I'll be glad when this is over. I feel sick!"

Mr Anderson laughed. "I bet. Some of these fences are quite difficult. Are you sure Honey can manage them?"

"No. That's *why* I feel sick. But I'm going to do my best to get her over them."

"Good for you. Can you remember it now?"

"Yes, I hope so."

They'd walked through the wooded part again and Amber counted them off: seven – gate into wood; eight – *huge* log pile; nine – tyres; ten – scary trakehner; eleven – wall out into the field. They'd just got out of the wood when they heard a whistle being blown and a few seconds later the first Open rider came soaring out over the wall. She had let her reins slip and was leaning back. It was then that Amber noticed the ground on the landing side was much lower than the take-off, making quite a substantial drop. She gulped as a wave of doubt crashed over her. She really didn't know if she and Honey could do this. Although cross-country practice had gone well through the week, these extra fences were terrifying.

"They've started. Come on, we'd better get back and get you in the saddle. It won't be long now."

With legs like lead, Amber stumbled back to the warm-up area. She could see her mum holding Honey amidst the circling riders. She swooned as another gut-wrenching wave of anxiety washed over her. What had she been thinking of earlier when she'd felt she might have a chance of beating Elisha? She'd be lucky just to survive this course, never mind be placed. The log pile was huge and really wide, the ditch under the trakehner was black and scary and she'd never jumped an angled rail before, and there was the terrifying drop after the wall.

She barely had the strength to mount, and once seated in the saddle with her shortened stirrups, she felt so precarious and unstable - not at all the easy, comfortable way she usually felt on Honey.

"Good luck! We're going out on the course to watch. See you soon." Mrs Anderson patted Amber's leg and smiled up at her. The smile wavered and faltered as she made eye contact with her daughter and saw the worry on her pallid face.

As they walked away from their daughter, Carol Anderson turned to her husband and whispered fiercely, "She looks terrified, and I don't blame her, having to go round her first cross-country on our Honey, especially when she has an experienced jumping pony back at home. What's the course like? Only small?"

Mr Anderson pressed his lips together and shook his head. "No…I'd say it's a tough course. This place runs a lot of affiliated competitions and the course was professionally built. Some of the jumps are pretty imposing. They're mainly about eighty centimetres but they've put some of the nineties in too. I know she's particularly worried about the jumps in the wood, especially the wall with the big drop on the landing side."

"Oh my God," wailed Mrs Anderson. "I can't watch!"

-Fourteen-

A Ride to Remember

Amber watched as a boy called Ashley was called to the start box. The starter told him he had thirty seconds and then counted him down from five to 'go!' His blue-eyed piebald pony seemed to know what it was all about and leapt out of the start box as soon as the 'g' of 'go' was said. He tore off towards the first jump and flew it eagerly with ears pricked. Amber saw them take the next five fences in the field confidently before they disappeared into the wood. Riders were being started at two-minute intervals and soon the next one was being called to the start.

Amber was busy trying to breathe slowly and convince herself she wasn't going to faint when Natalie rode up alongside her. Rocky's red coat was already damp as he danced and shook his head savagely.

"I don't think he likes this bit," Natalie looked as ill as Amber felt and again, she wished she had made more effort to get Natalie on her own and warn her about Rocky. She was surprised and impressed that Natalie was going ahead with the cross-country phase after her disastrous attempt during the week. She doubted that she would've had the confidence if the same thing had happened to her

"What is it?" Amber didn't know much about bits as her ponies all wore snaffles.

"It's an American gag. He had a kimblewick earlier in the week, but I couldn't hold him, so Elisha's put him in this for the cross-country. She says it'll hold him, but he hates it."

Amber wasn't surprised that he didn't approve of any braking system that would stop him running amok and make him do what the rider wanted instead of having his own way.

"Are you nervous?" Natalie's big round brown eyes looked bigger and darker than ever against her lightly grey skin.

"It's a very real possibility that I'll puke when they call me to the start," Amber admitted.

"Oh, me too!" Natalie looked relieved to find Amber shared her fear. "Elisha said I was stupid to be worried 'cause Rocky's done Opens and he'll find this so easy. I'm terrified I don't go clear in case she thinks I'm useless!"

Amber was just about to tell Natalie that she shouldn't worry about what Elisha said when Natalie's name was called by a steward and she didn't get the chance.

"Natalie Riley. Come to the start please."

"Oh no!" The poor girl looked truly stricken.

"Good luck… and be careful," Amber called as Natalie trotted away. She received a faint nod in reply.

Rocky left the start box like a rocket, just like the piebald pony who had since galloped strongly through the finish and was enveloped in a delighted hug by his red-faced rider. Like the piebald, Rocky cleared the first six fences and was soon out of sight.

Kate was called to the start on Breeze and Amber's stomach twisted painfully as she realised it would soon be her turn. The heavy lump that had been sliding slowly down her throat suddenly seemed to get stuck and threatened to choke her. She knew that she would be sick if she had to wait much longer, so she gave Honey one more jump over the practice fence and headed for the steward to present herself.

"You're keen! Coming without being called. Or is it a case of wanting to get it over with?" The steward was one of the centre's grooms. She was only about twenty and had a very friendly face. She smiled kindly at Amber. "Just go out and enjoy it, that's what you're here for. In five minutes, you'll be back and wondering what all the worry was about."

Amber trembled in response. She just wanted to get started before she lost her nerve, but there seemed to be some hold on the course. Something must have happened to either Natalie or Kate. The wait was torturous as Amber fretted about what was causing the hold up, but eventually the starter beckoned her to come over.

"Good luck!" Amber heard a yell and saw Emily standing in her stirrups on Fudge, waving at her absurdly with both arms above her head like a mayday signal. The sight made her laugh and suddenly she felt slightly more cheerful. She had to pull herself together for Honey's sake. As wonderful as she'd been this week, the little blip in the show jumping had shown she couldn't do it on her own. She needed Amber to be a rider, not a passenger who was a bag of nerves.

"Thirty seconds."

Her insides did a loop-the-loop and the lump in her throat made itself comfortable. She rode into the start box, closed her eyes and inhaled deeply, letting the breath out slowly and shakily as she opened her eyes and gathered up her reins, seeing Honey's pricked black ears ahead of her like the sights of a gun.

"Five…four…three…two…one…go! Good luck!"

Honey set off and got into canter immediately. She jumped the brush fence happily and took the barrels and tree stumps in her stride. Next was the open ditch, in practice just a gash in the ground, but now it was flanked on either side by a child-sized wooden carving of a bear. Amber felt Honey check and slow down as she spotted the terrible monsters. "Come on girl!" she urged and gave Honey a light tap with the whip. The pony approached hesitantly with popping eyes and twisted her body as she jumped the ditch as if worried one of the bears might take a swipe at her as she passed between them

"Good lass!" Amber gave her a pat and rode strongly over the Irish bank and double of logs. With adrenaline now coursing through her, Amber's nerves were completely forgotten as she approached the gate into the wood. The large Open gate had been replaced with a lower one, but she remembered the possible problem of jumping from light into the shade of the trees and pushed on. Honey jumped neatly into the leafy cool of the wood and followed the soft, slightly churned path to the log pile. It was the widest jump on the course and Amber knew that jumping width was Honey's biggest weakness. Praying she could make it, Amber kicked on, hoping against hope that with a good run up the momentum would be enough to get them over.

Honey felt her rider's determination and it gave her confidence. She measured the jump up quickly, gathered herself and made a huge effort. Her hind feet just clipped the top as she stretched out to land, but it didn't bother her and they both had a moment to catch their breath over an easy tyre jump.

The next fence was another rider frightener – the trakehner – a wide black ditch with a heavy telegraph pole angled across it. Amber had been very unsure about this fence, but Emily had told her the angle of the pole didn't matter as the pony wouldn't notice it and she should aim for the middle. Amber rode strongly again, but Honey wasn't too sure about this new jump and wanted to get a good look at it.

"*Please* don't stop," Amber pleaded as Honey dropped out of canter into trot. "Go on!"

Honey lowered her head and assessed the jump suspiciously while Amber pushed her on. By the time they reached take-off point, Honey was moving painfully slowly, and Amber was sure she was going to stop. "*Hup*," she cried sharply, and deciding to do as she was told, Honey jumped awkwardly twisting her body in the air.

Thump. As they landed, Amber missed the middle of the saddle and lost her right stirrup. Clinging on desperately she wriggled back from her lopsided position and frantically searched for her stirrup with her foot. By now the wall fence was right in front of her. If she pulled up now, she knew she would be given a refusal but if she jumped like this, out of balance because of the lost stirrup, with the drop on the other side, she would fall off and get even more penalties.

It was too late to pull out now.

As she felt Honey begin to take off, she kicked her left foot out so that she had no stirrups. It was a risk but at least her balance was equal. She gripped with her legs as tightly as she could. Going over the jump was like a slow-motion replay. As they reached the point just before the descent to landing, Amber looked down. The ground seemed a long way off. As Honey's front end began to tilt forward, Amber felt like she was on a rollercoaster, strapped in looking over the bar just before plummeting, screaming to the ground. Her stomach lurched just as if she *was* on a rollercoaster as they plunged forward. Remembering seeing the girl in the Open class at this fence, she leaned back as far as she could, letting her reins slip so that she didn't jab Honey in the mouth. It seemed to take an age to land but when they did, the impact jolted Amber out of the saddle and she slipped round to the right.

"Aaaarrghh! Honey, wait!" Obediently, the pony slowed while Amber scrambled back into the saddle and pushed her hat up from over her eyes.

"Phew, that was close!" She composed herself, regained her stirrups and patted Honey. They'd cleared the biggest fences on the course, but it wasn't over yet. "Come on lass, let's finish this!"

But Honey was tired now. The big jumps in the wood had taken it out of her and there were still six to go. She kept going but Amber knew she had little left to give and didn't push her. Fortunately, the three steps were jumped downhill and didn't require as much effort as going up them. They trotted through the coffin and the water jump and over the straw bales until there were only two fences left. The penultimate fence was a white house. It had a black door and windows painted on and even had a peaked roof.

"Don't give up, we're nearly home," Amber implored.

Honey's head was low now, but always wanting to please, she cleared the house so that only the last – a chair fence festooned with brightly coloured flowers – stood between them and the finish. Honey saw it and checked. She didn't like the look of those flowers and she was so tired. But Amber was calling to her, willing her to go on. She wasn't going to repeat her mistake from the show jumping of not riding the final fence.

"Please Honey, only one more!"

And so, Honey made one last super effort and somehow got to the other side of the last jump on the course.

Euphoria like she had never known engulfed Amber as they trotted wearily through the finish flags. She jumped straight off Honey and hugged her tightly. The pony was streaming with sweat and rivulets were running down her face and dripping from her eyelids. She was tired out but as Amber pulled a Polo mint out of her jodhpur pocket and offered it to her, she could see how alive Honey looked. Her eyes were shining, and she looked...what was it?

Proud.

As she stood there crunching her mint, engulfed in a warm cloud of steam, Amber could see she had changed. She wasn't Honey the nervous riding school pony who always went at the back anymore. She was Honey who had just got a clear round! Amber stood and let it sink in. This was real, it had actually happened. She knew she would remember this moment for the rest of her life.

Amber slacked the girth, pulled the reins over Honey's head and began to lead her back to the stables. She was tempted to wait as Emily was out on the course now and would soon be back, but she thought Honey would appreciate getting her tack off and having a nice hose down with cold water to wash away the sweat.

As she walked past the warm-up area, she saw Chelsea on her grey pony heading towards the start. Elisha, at present the top placed competitor, was the only rider left. But if there had been another hundred riders, she would still have been unmissable. Elisha wore white breeches and a white shirt under a banana yellow body protector. Her hat cover was royal blue with yellow stars and pompom. Thunder Cat looked magnificent; his yellow bandages making him look even blacker.

Pulling herself up straight and holding her head high, Amber walked past her, wondering, and hoping, *Will she ask the question*? Sure enough, Elisha trotted up alongside her and called, "She looks tired. Too much for her was it?"

Amber knew that was what Elisha was expecting, since she seemed to believe Fell ponies were completely incapable of anything. She stopped and smiled to herself, savouring the moment, before looking up into Elisha's cold, hard stare. Meeting her gaze unflinchingly, she said,

171

"Yes, she is tired. It wasn't easy for her, only being a Fell pony from a riding school… but we went clear."

"Oh." Elisha tried not to let her feelings show but she was too slow to regain her icy smile for Amber to miss her change of expression. "Well…well done." For once, she looked away first.

"Thanks!" Amber said brightly, bursting with joy. She knew it had probably nearly killed Elisha to say that to her, but she'd had to. What else could she have said?

"Good luck for your round!" she called cheerily over her shoulder.

And leaving Elisha frowning behind her, she walked away, leading her pony with the biggest grin on her face and the best feeling she'd ever had in her life. Not only had Honey been fantastic; she was also impressed with her own bravery in tackling such a tough course. And then there was the cherry on the cake, of course; she had finally stood up for herself and left Elisha lost for words. She actually felt *proud* of herself for once and she revelled in the unfamiliar feeling. It was like wearing new clothes …like a new Amber had emerged.

-Fifteen-

Not Second Best

Riders and parents assembled in the classroom. All the action was over, the ponies were relaxing in their stables and everything had been tidied, ready for packing up and going home in the morning. All everyone wanted to know was the result of the One Day Event, although many people already had a good idea of the placings in their class.

The classroom had all the tables and chairs pushed to the edges of the room leaving a large empty floor area in the middle. The tables were piled high with all kinds of delicious party foods and drinks in preparation for the last night of camp.

Mrs Best entered the room carrying a large tray of rosettes. "Okay folks, are we all ready?"

Silence fell and everyone looked eagerly towards the DC in her green wool suit as she beamed happily at everyone.

"Well, here we are! The week is almost over, and it is my pleasure to be here to present the awards tonight. Let's begin with the Novice class."

One by one the riders from the Novice class came out to collect their rosettes while everyone clapped, and they blushed.

"And now we have our Intermediate riders. This was the most exciting class, with the cross-country proving very influential." Mrs Best seemed to be bubbling with excitement. She was like a child surrounded by presents on Christmas morning. "In first place with a score of forty-four, and the only rider to finish on their dressage score is Emily Pryde on Freaky Treacle!" The room erupted with applause as Emily went forward to collect her rosette and trophy. "In second place, with fifty-four after an unfortunate refusal on the cross-country is Chelsea Connor and Skylark." More polite applause. "And in third with a terrific clear in the cross-country, but with eight time penalties is Amber Anderson and Townend Honeysuckle!"

The results continued with Ashley moving up to fourth, thanks to his clear round cross-country after having two fences down in the show jumping and being last in the dressage. There were whoops and cheers for Ashley, who rode Bandit, a piebald cob with feathers and a serious moustache that his father also used as a driving pony. He was shocking at the dressage but loved charging round the cross-country and was surprisingly nimble for a part-time carthorse. The final rosette went to Kate who was pleased with her fifth place on the young and inexperienced Breeze.

Natalie had fallen off at the wall that nearly claimed Amber. She hadn't been expecting the drop on the landing side, having not seen it, and wasn't prepared to lean back to help keep her balance. She'd just been tipped off and Rocky had gone for a nice run around the field on his own before someone caught him and reunited him with Natalie. Sadly, because of the fall, she was not allowed to remount and continue but despite this, she'd had a great time as Rocky had flown everything for her and she'd only fallen off because of her own lack of balance.

Amber had sympathy for her; she knew that she too would have ended up on the ground at that fence if Honey hadn't stopped to allow her to get back into the saddle. Natalie's dad had been on the phone with Elisha's dad and agreed that they would be buying Rocky as soon as Sable could be sold.

A boy called Jake had also been eliminated on the cross-country: for missing a fence out. He was gutted as he thought he'd gone clear and would've been well placed otherwise. His misfortune confirmed to Amber that her decision to go back and look at the course again had been the right one.

As for Elisha, who was conspicuous by her absence at the prize giving, she had finished, for the first time in her life, in equal last place after being eliminated on the cross-country. Somehow, she had managed to get Thunder Cat, after more than one attempt, over the first ditch, the trakehner and the coffin, but the water proved to be their undoing again. Elisha had tried to wear spurs, but the centre's staff had made her take them off as she didn't have a note from the DC giving her permission to wear them. So, when Thunder Cat had skittered and stopped at the water, she'd had a temper tantrum and whipped him fiercely, screaming and lashing hysterically. At that point, the manager of the centre – a tall, serious horseman – had marched angrily across the field, bawled at Elisha until she actually cried, took her whip off her and threw it in the water jump before leading her off the course. She hadn't been seen since.

Natalie confided to Amber and Emily that Elisha had phoned her dad and told him her version of events and that he was coming to take her and the horses away later that night. Although Amber felt no fondness for the girl, she did feel a brief moment of sympathy for her, now sitting alone in her horsebox instead of joining in the party with everyone else.

"Here you go." Emily appeared with a beaker of something fizzy for Amber, with Natalie shyly remaining with them now that Elisha wasn't there. Emily raised her cup in a toast and Amber playfully joined in, bashing her plastic cup against Emily's.

"Here's to our success." Emily grinned. "And to the best part of the week – beating Elisha!"

Amber sipped her drink thoughtfully. She had, unbelievably, managed to achieve the unreachable dream of defeating Elisha. A sense of peace and contentment hugged her. But was that truly the reason for her happiness? The recent events flashed through her mind like a silent movie. Watching the replay was electrifying and thrilled her each time she re-lived it. She smiled to herself, remembering crossing the finish with a clear round behind her.

"I can see you smiling," Emily teased. "I told you we had a chance to beat Elisha and you didn't believe me. Feels good eh?"

"Yes, but that wasn't why I was smiling."

"No? Then what?"

Slowly, knowing how she felt inside but not knowing how to put it into words, Amber tried to explain. "It's funny, but after all the things Elisha has said to me and all the time I've spent wishing I could beat her, now it's happened I'm not even bothered."

Emily's eyebrows leapt up her forehead as her eyes widened in surprise.

"You're not bothered? What do you mean? Why not?"

"Well, I feel so happy now it's unbelievable, but I would still have felt like this if Elisha had won...although obviously it's much better that you won," she added quickly. "It's just that it doesn't matter to me now about other people. If everyone else had done better and I'd ended up last in our group, I'd still be over the moon because I know I couldn't have done any better, apart from that silly mistake in the show jumping. I was terrified of the cross-country course, but I got round it clear. And what's even better about it is that it wasn't on a ready-made competition pony that I could just point at the fences and know I was getting over them. It was on a pony nobody expected anything of. I brought her here as the second best pony because the trophy winner couldn't come, and despite having no experience, she gave me everything she had. I'll never forget this week. It's let me see that winning isn't everything."

"Wow, well I don't think everyone would agree with you. Elisha for one."

"Well, that's her loss. If you have to win to be happy, it'll probably add up to a pretty disappointing life. You can't win all the time, as she's just discovered."

"Man, that's profound. You've got a wise head on those shoulders for one so young." Emily chuckled and shook her head in wonder, pulling Amber and Natalie into a hug. "But I did win and all I can say is, it made me *very* happy! I may never do it again so let's make the most of it."

Just then, a loud party tune started to play on the centre's loudspeakers.

"Come on girls, let's dance." Emily strutted into the middle of the room, dragging a giggling Amber and a very reluctant Natalie with her.

**

The next morning everybody loaded up their ponies and everything they'd brought, ready to head home. Natalie had gone the previous evening with Elisha when her dad came to get her, since Natalie had been sleeping in the luxurious living quarters of Elisha's horsebox with her all week. Amber waved as first Kate, then Chelsea then Ashley and Jake were driven from the yard by their parents, until there was only Emily left.

"We can wait with you 'til your parents get here," Mrs Anderson said to Emily.

"Oh no, it's fine - you go. Mum's just texted to say they're five minutes away. You'd better go now so you don't bump into them on the lane," Emily answered casually.

Mrs Anderson nodded and went back to the car and got in with her husband who was sitting waiting. Honey was already loaded in the trailer, waiting to begin the journey back to Shaw Farm.

"Well, I'll see you then, probably at school on Monday." Amber gave Emily a shy hug. "Thanks for everything this week. I've had the best time."

Emily ruffled her hair in the way adults often do to small boys. "It was great. Our second rate ponies didn't do so bad, did they?" she joked.

"Nothing second rate or second best about them."

"You're right about that," Emily agreed, somewhat solemnly. Amber couldn't understand why Emily didn't look happier when she said this. "So, you'd better get going. Like I said, you don't want to meet my parents on the lane. Two vehicles can't pass on it and it's a long way to reverse with a trailer on." Emily seemed keen to get Amber into her car.

"Okay. See you soon then." Amber opened the car door and got into the back seat.

"Yeah, bye!"

They drove away, leaving Emily waving behind them. Just as they got to the end of the lane, an old battered 4x4 turned in pulling a slightly shabby trailer behind it.

"Emily was right, we've just escaped bumping into her parents," Mrs Anderson said happily.

When Amber looked at the other car, however, there was only one person in it – a woman driver with unruly dark hair like Emily's. Emily had seemed to think both her parents would be coming to pick her up, but it looked like her dad hadn't been able to make it.

Thinking no more of it, Amber settled back into her seat and slipped into a daydream in which she was riding the cross-country course of the previous day again on Honey. She really couldn't think of any experience she'd had that had been as scary, thrilling and wonderful all at the same time. It was, she thought, the best moment of her life so far. *May there be many more,* she hoped as they headed back to the farm and to Molly and Pearl who were there waiting for them.

The Perfect Pony for Me

By Ashtyn Wade

That horse won.
We all knew he would;
The £18,000 imported horse
Who dominated the course.

My tiny Fell pony came in second,
But she's better I reckon.
No, she's not as tall,
But she can still do it all.

You see, my little Fell pony,
She jumped everything, and nothing felt funny.
She was the star,
Flying faster than a car.

She flew higher than a hawk,
And that time she clocked –
I'm proud of my pony,
Way better than any phony.

So, my Fell came in second,
To your expensive Christmas present.
But my Fell pony is first,
In heart, skill, and effort, she means the most.

Author's Note

"There is no secret so close as between a
rider and his horse."
~ R. S. Surtees

Helen and Honey, Greystoke Castle, 1993

Honey was a revelation to me and taught me a lot about underestimation.

When we first got Honey, she was frightened of everything: literally a bag of nerves. I think she was a timid personality, and being a riding school pony, she couldn't get confidence from her riders, who were often novices, so she took it from being part of the herd. She was always part of a large group that went out on rides together, so when we got her, and expected her to go out with just Pearl for company, she couldn't see how she could possibly be expected to manage this dangerous task and tried very hard for a long time to avoid it. The lessons I learned about ponies began right from that first day, when we couldn't even get them to leave the yard of their new home as neither was used to being the lead pony. There began my real-world instruction in patience, perseverance, and trying to see the world through the eyes of a pony.

We did eventually manage to get the pair of them going out almost happily together, though Honey would never take the lead. Beside Pearl instead of behind her was the best she could manage.

So, the thought that this cowardly pony would ever become a Pony Club star never occurred to any of us. How could a pony who couldn't hack out on her own due to all the scary things waiting to kill her (she thought) go around a cross-country course, all alone, jumping solid, imposing fences?

I suppose it was because she, unlike Pearl, absolutely loved jumping, and I hope, because she came to trust me as her rider. Honey was the first pony with whom I shared the fear and exhilaration of riding cross-country. There is nothing like it for creating a bond between pony and rider, and I was hooked.

Jumping was Honey's hidden talent, and it brought out her personality and confidence. She regularly went clear round all the cross-country courses in our local area, back in the days when there was a hunter trials season. When other riders were struggling to get over deep scary ditches or through the brown, muddy water jump, my little scaredy cat jumped everything in sight. It really did seem like a miracle, and every time we came back clear, we all struggled to believe it.

I had thought that because Pearl didn't like jumping, neither would Honey or any other Fell pony, for that matter. But Honey taught us that all ponies are individuals, regardless of their breed.

She wasn't the fastest and her stamina often let her down towards the end of a round, but she gave me *everything* she had and for that, I loved her and could ask no more.

Acknowledgements

My first thanks go to the lovely readers of *Little Pearl* who contacted me directly or left reviews on Amazon to share their reactions to the book. I've had some really positive feedback and it's wonderful to hear from people who have enjoyed it. Particularly thrilling was hearing from World Champion Ros Canter and award-winning author Sheena Wilkinson; I'm grateful to them for taking the time to read the book and contact me about it.

Similarly, thank you to the beta readers of *The Second Best Pony* for your thoughts on the unedited proof version of the story. Your support and comments were positive, constructive and much appreciated.

To those who entered the 'cover star competition' to find a pony model to represent Honey on the cover of this book, I loved seeing all your beautiful ponies. I looked at them all every day for weeks, wondering how they could be narrowed down to one eventual winner, but in the end … Greenholme Clyde owned by Katie Trotter was voted number one. *Let's Get Booked* then used the image (permission granted by L Meader Photography) to create the book's stunning cover and also helped me to edit and refine the story. Thank you, Amanda, for helping me clarify my intentions for this book.

To the winners of the illustration and poetry competitions linked to this book: thank you for your creativity. The illustration on the dedication page is by 14-year-old Abbie Wilkins, who loves drawing animals and is a talented artist. I'm honoured to have a piece of her art in my book. The poem, *The Perfect Pony for Me,* at the end of the book was written by Ashtyn Wade, also 14 years-old. She wrote the poem without having read *The Second Best Pony* and I thought it was uncanny how her words reflected the sentiment of the story. It was perfect for inclusion in the book. I love working creatively with young people and to have young writers and artists getting involved with my work means a lot.

And finally, thanks again to my husband for being so supportive and for being the final proof reader. There's always something he spots that no-one else has seen!

About the Author

Helen has been horse-mad all her life. Her adventures with ponies began back in 1990 with Pearl and Honey, but they are still continuing now with her three horses, Maddy, Charlie and Holly who are all just as interesting and individual as Pearl and Honey were, and will probably end up in a book in the future too! Watch out for them.

Maddy is quite like Pearl: full of personality and mischief. She has got herself into more trouble over the years than all the rest of the horses put together. Maddy enjoyed Riding Club activities for many years and has done everything from British Eventing to Pony Club games. She's a real fun horse who is now semi-retired, but still enjoys hacking out.

Then there's Charlie, AKA the Ginger Tank who thinks he's a thoroughbred racehorse but was sadly born into the body of a draft horse. He loves jumping, beach rides and charging about on cross-country courses.

Finally, there's Holly, the sensitive girl who is a sweet swot – always wanting to get things right – with an anxious side.

When Helen isn't busy writing books or playing with horses, she is also a secondary school librarian and English teacher. Just as well as the loves of her life are reading, writing and riding!

She lives in Cumbria with her husband, horses and a variety of dogs, hens, ducks and geese!

Visit www.helenharaldsen.co.uk to find out more about Helen, her books and her horses.

You can also sign up to the mailing list to receive news, competitions and opportunities liked to Helen's books, as well as free bonus *Amber's Pony Tales* content– available exclusively to subscribers

Did you enjoy this book? The author would love to see your reviews on Amazon.

Please feel free to post your comments and let others know about Amber's Pony Tales.
You can also follow Amber's Pony Tales on Facebook.

Read the next book in the series, *Trusting Molly*, to find out if Amber can find the key that will allow her to connect with Molly. Will she ever regain her confidence in the talented but unpredictable pony? Read Book 3 to find out.

Printed in Great Britain
by Amazon

67432389R00121